I0733650

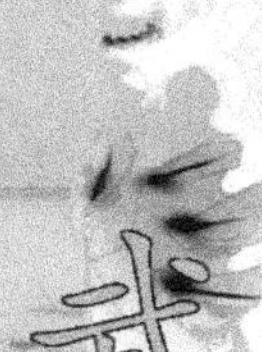
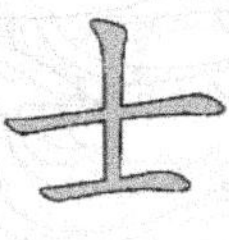

FIGHTING UPSTREAM

BOOK TWO OF THE BUSHIDO CHRONICLES

JASON BRICK

Published in the United States by
Not a Pipe Publishing, Independence, Oregon.
www.NotAPipePublishing.com

Paperback Edition

ISBN-13: 978-1-956892-36-9

Dedication

This is for my wife and sons.

FIGHTING UPSTREAM

BOOK 2 OF
THE BUSHIDO CHRONICLES

Chapter 1

I'd made it to Friday.

At the Oregon State Wrestling Championships, competitions start on a Thursday. If you lose two matches, you're out. Everybody still in it on Friday has won at least once, and has a shot at a medal on Saturday. A shot at a medal as a sophomore meant a shot at a scholarship two years later. A shot at a scholarship meant a shot at a better life for me and Mom.

So making it to Friday was good news. The bad news was who I had to wrestle that morning.

His name was, and I'm not kidding, Angus Brawn. Angus was way over six feet tall, with long arms and legs that looked like knotted ropes. Every pound on him was muscle. I'd wrestled him before, and he was stronger than me. Plus he was a senior, with more experience, and more to lose because this would be his last high school tournament ever.

I'd lost to him by two points last January, but I promised myself I would reverse that this time. Looking at him warm up on the opposite side of the bright red mat, I wasn't sure how well I could keep that promise.

Sage Kaiser, a 185-pound varsity wrestler on my team and one of my best friends in the world, slapped me on the butt and whispered to me, "Bring me one of his ears." I laughed.

She said, "No. Seriously. You come off that mat and he has both his ears, I'm eating your lunch." She slapped me on the butt again. I glanced up into the seats of the auditorium, where my girlfriend Susan was sitting with Fiel, Galhardo, and Alex. I hoped she hadn't seen that.

Coach Russell clapped me on the shoulder and said, "You know what to do." I jumped up and down on my left leg. It twinged a little, running lines of pain up my leg and into my stomach. Less than two months ago, a powerful demon had nearly broken it and stabbed it with shards from a dinner plate. But with the help of Alex and Fiel and Galhardo's *vovo*, it healed so quickly my doctor was writing a paper about it. It would hold.

I walked out. Behind me, coach shouted, "Go get him, Morgan!"

The second I put my foot on the mat, Angus shuffled to his line and stopped moving. He stood like a statue. A statue of granite I would wrestle in less than a minute. I took my place opposite him and reached out my hand to shake. He slapped it away with a contemptuous snort.

That was weird. Angus had roundly kicked my butt in our first match together, but he'd been a good sport. He had a reputation for it.

"Make him eat that hand, Connor Morgan!" a woman's voice shouted from just off the mat. It might have been Sage, but was probably Mom. The ref blew the whistle.

Angus headbutted me before the sound was over. He raked his forehead across my nose and eyes as we grabbed each other by the backs of our necks. The position is called *tying up*, and is common in heavyweight wrestling. The headbutt was a bonus.

While I was still seeing stars, Angus dropped low and grabbed both my legs for a takedown. I had just enough sense to shoot my feet back and drop my weight on the back of his head. We struggled that way for what seemed like an hour, but couldn't have been longer than two minutes. The buzzer sounded with the score 0-0.

I ran back to the starting lines, my legs feeling bands of pain from where Angus's arms had dug into them. He was stronger than I remembered, and I'd remembered him being really, really strong.

I won the coin toss and chose bottom position. I set up on my hands and knees. Angus took his place above and behind me, crushing me with his weight and grinding his fingers into the nerves at my elbow.

When the whistle blew, I grabbed Angus's hand and rolled forward, taking him with me and landing with him beneath me on his back. He bucked and squirmed while I held his arm and tried to get a solid hold on his legs with my other hand. I couldn't hold him flat long enough to get the pin, but the ref called out two points for the reversal, then three for the near fall. I was winning, 5-0.

I glanced at coach to see if I should let him go and try for more points, but Angus's huge hand slapped right over the top of my face. His fingers dug into my temples and eyes as he wrenched me backward. He rolled us both then, slamming me face-first onto the mat. I didn't see what hit me in the back of the head but felt the rocking impact just as the whistle blew for the end of the second round.

Coach Russell shouted the ref's name. He might have used other words, too, but I wasn't hearing at my best. My head hurt and I felt dizzy as I stumbled over toward him. Mom was there, too. She shined a penlight into my eyes while making worried clucking noises with her mouth.

"Kicking him," Sage was muttering to coach. "I should..."

Mom worked as an ER nurse, and was picking up extra money working as a medic for the tournament, which let her come watch me wrestle without missing a paycheck from her hospital shifts.

"No concussion," she said to coach. To me, she said, "You're all right, Connor."

"Aw, mom," I said.

"Aw, mom," said coach. He nodded his head in the direction of the mat, then took me by the shoulders.

I glanced above his head, looking into the stands until I found Susan. She looked worried, and my friends around her looked angry. Coach spun me to face Angus, who was prowling and smiling at his side of the mat. Sage whispered in my ear, using my other name. "Watch out, *Chuugi*. Angus doesn't fight dirty. Something's going on."

A wave of fear ran from my gut to my throat then. The demons my friends and I fought could possess people, make them do terrible things. They had made us fight our classmates before we drove them out of our high school. If one had taken over Angus, I was in for a rough time.

I nodded, then jogged up to the line. Angus chose both up for our final round, starting us facing one another like we had when the match started. The whistle blew and Angus broke my nose with a palm heel to my face.

It was blatant, and the ref blew the whistle immediately. That kind of intentional hitting is an automatic disqualification. Gasps and angry shouts sounded at the edge of the mat.

But I relaxed. The match was over. Mom, or maybe Alex, would patch me up and I would advance to my next match, that much closer to a medal. My nose hurt, but it was worth it.

Except Angus wasn't finished.

He grabbed my wrist in one hand even though the match was over, and dropped his body to drape me over his shoulders in a fireman's carry. Then he stood up and lifted me as easily as if I were wrestling at 126 pounds.

"Brawn!" the ref shouted.

"Angus! What the hell are you doing?" another voice said.

Angus ignored both. He lifted me above his head with a move only a supernatural being would be strong enough to do, and shifted my body to his front. Then he dropped me spine-first onto his bent knee, breaking my back.

Pain exploded through my entire body. It felt like I was suddenly on fire everywhere, all at once. It hurt so much I couldn't see. I could feel myself screaming in my throat and chest, but couldn't hear it through the pain. Then my vision cleared, and the pain went away.

So did everything else. I found myself on the ground with the sounds of fighting somewhere out of my vision. I tried to turn my head to see what was happening, but it didn't move. I tried again. Nothing happened.

I couldn't move my head at all.

I couldn't move my arms or legs, either. Then I realized my lungs weren't moving. I wasn't breathing. I *couldn't* breathe. The pressure in them built, and continued to build, as they burned from lack of oxygen my body did nothing to relieve.

I stared straight up at the lights of the stadium, willing my breath to come, but it wouldn't obey. Then Mom's face came into my vision.

If I thought I'd been afraid before, I was wrong. Fear for Mom flooded through me as I realized what she must be feeling, but something in her expression told me not to worry. There was no sadness in her face, no fear, just a fierce and cold focus.

Mom was in her zone now, focused on saving my life. She didn't have the luxury of being scared or sad. Her lips moved, but her words got lost in the rush of blood in my ears. An EMT knelt down on the opposite side of me.

They worked together on something below the bottom of my vision.

"I'm sorry, Mom," I tried to say. But of course I could only *think it,* because my mouth didn't work. I tried to think it as loudly as I could so maybe a part of her would hear me.

I felt a pressure in my throat then, and a soft, white glow entered the bottom of my vision. A sphere, about the size of my closed fist, rose upward out of my mouth. It looked like a pearl, with smoky markings in the shape of the Japanese symbol for *chuugi,* for loyalty, for my name. It was my Bushido spirit, the source of the powers that made me part of the shadow war of which I had just become a casualty.

The pearl that only left a Bushido Warrior when their fight was over for good.

That was it, then. No more wrestling. No more fighting the good fight alongside my friends. No more kissing Susan in her car in front of my apartment. No more bad movies and good pizza nights with Mom.

Her eyes went wide just then, as she realized what I already knew. I thought *I love you* to her as loudly as I could. It was all I had left to do for her, so it's what I did. And then...

...and then I died.

Chapter 2

"Connor!" Mom shouted from the dining room table. "L minus ten minutes!"

I didn't know what L stood for, but I knew she was calling me to breakfast. I finished putting my deodorant on, then bent a little so I could see my head stubble in the mirror. I wasn't looking good, but I was looking ready.

"Coming!" I walked the five steps from the bathroom to the card table we'd set up in the half of our living room closest to the kitchen bar.

Mom was at the table, a plate and a pile of mail in front of her. Most of the mail was in those pink envelopes that meant overdue bills, and her plate was about half full of a fluffy, white thing that smelled like garlic and fat.

Beside her sat *Vovo*, the grandmother of my friends and fellow demon hunters Fiel and Galhardo. She'd helped get my injured leg back into fighting shape, and had given it one last check before I was allowed to shower and get ready for the tournament. Mrs. Dochevnya, our elderly downstairs neighbor, stood behind her filling a plate with more of the fully-white-garlic-fat stuff. She smiled at me, her whole face wrinkling, and gestured with a loaded spoon.

"Eat, strange boy. Today is big day."

She was right. Thursday morning, this morning, was the beginning of the Oregon State Wrestling Championships. Coach Russell had told me I was beginning to get attention from college scouts even though it was just my sophomore year. If I could win a medal on Saturday, or even stay in the running until Friday, it would help me get a scholarship to college. If I got to go to college, I could get a good job. If I could get a good job, I could take better care of Mom. If I could take better care of Mom, she wouldn't have to live in an apartment so small we had to pretend to have a dining room.

I sat down, and put a fork in the fluffy food. It might have been egg whites, or potatoes, or both, and it had lumps of some kind of spicy protein mixed into it. I scooped some into my mouth. It was heavenly, but I only ate four bites , then put my fork down.

"Mrs. D, this is amazing," I said. To Mom, I said, "Does L stand for *let's get ready?*"

Mom just shook her head, smiling a little. Mrs. D shook a finger at me. "Eat, strange boy."

"I ate," I said. "I'm eating. See?" I took another small bite, loving the taste even while the heavy food settled in my stomach like...well, like a bunch of eggs, potatoes, grease, and spices settling into the belly of somebody who had to wrestle in a couple of hours.

Vovo took her side, "You need your strength today, *neto.*"

"I need to move like I don't have three pounds of yummy, yummy concrete in my body."

Vovo laughed, the chuckle running through her whole body and shaking it. Mrs. D fixed me with the kind of look that let me know why they used to say witches have the evil eye, and she wasn't even a witch.

Well, she probably wasn't, but she had driven a demon out of me once using only a walking stick and some table salt.

"Mom, does L stand for *laughing?*"

Mom just shook her head. Mrs. D said, "I will pack you some for later." Then she loaded up a plastic bowl with what was left on my plate. She and *Vovo* got up and went out our front door, speaking in a language I didn't recognize but could tell was neither Mrs. D's native Ukrainian or *Vovo's* Portuguese.

"*Lifetime achievement?*" I said to mom as the door swung shut between the two women.

"Nope."

I went to my room to grab my gym bag. I paused for a moment, surveying the posters on my wall. Legendary wrestlers Dan Gable, Cael Sanderson, and Kyle Maynard looked back at me. "All right, guys. Wish me luck," I said to them.

Luck is not a factor, I heard in my mind as I walked back into the living room. When I got back out, Mom tried to hide a piece of paper under her plate.

"What's that?"

"Love letter," Mom said. "Lust letter, really. You don't want to read it."

"A lust letter from our landlord?"

"Hey, young man. How I pay our rent is none of your business."

"Augh! Mom! Don't even joke about that!" she laughed and tossed a wadded-up paper towel at me.

"Who says I'm joking? You still want to know what it says?"

I stopped smiling and said, "Yeah."

"Don't worry about it," Mom said, her face growing serious again.

"But *you're* worrying about it. I can tell. Which means I'm going to worry about it whether you tell me or not. I recommend you tell me, so at least while I'm worrying I'll also be thinking about how to solve whatever's going on."

Mom looked at me the way she sometimes does, her face wrinkled and smiling in a mixture of surprise and pride. "Sometimes, you talk more like an adult than the people at work. And you're right. You're no kid anymore."

"You got that straight. Are you going to show me?"

"Don't get cocky. You'll always be *my* kid. But here, if you want to see it." She handed me the letter. "It's L minus three, Connor." Outside, a horn honked in a short pattern of long and quick beeps. It was my friends, using our code to say everything is all right and it's really them.

"L stands for *late*, doesn't it?" I said.

Mom smiled and nodded, picking up her coffee mug, the one that said *Good Morning, Mom* on it.

"Can I take this with me, and read it later?"

"Yes. Go ahead."

"Okay. Love you, mom. See you, there?"

"Yes, son. Love you, too."

I headed out the door.

CHAPTER 3

I usually rode my bike to school. It was sort of a trademark for me, and I was proud of winning matches after riding three miles, or pumping out the return trip after a practice that exhausted everybody else. But today was different. Today I would need everything I had.

In our parking lot at the bottom of the stairs was Alex's blue Subaru hatchback. I could see her and Sage in the front seats, leaving room in the back for me to slide in with Fiel and Galhardo. Alex said, "Hey,

Chuugi," as I closed the door. Sage held her fist up and back over her seat for me to bump.

Galhardo and Fiel stared at me without saying a word. They kept staring as Alex put her car into gear. As we left my parking lot, Galhardo reached out across his brother and poked my shoulder with one finger of his good hand. He was born with only limited use of his right hand and leg, and usually used a cane to walk around. Despite that, he was an aikido expert and champion fencer. He fought the demons as well as any of us, and won at least as often.

"He's real," Galhardo said in a voice like a little kid meeting a real, live superhero.

"A *reaaal* wrestling champion," Fiel said. A bright smile creased his brown face, in a perfect mirror image of his brother.

"Ignore those two, Morgan," Sage called out from the front. "They did the same thing to me. Besides, they're early." The brothers broke out into laughter. Alex laughed, too, while Sage just started her playlist. Within moments, they were all singing along with *Bohemian Rhapsody* as the hatchback crawled through Portland morning traffic. I mouthed along for a while, then pulled out the letter Mom had been reading.

Like she said, it was from our landlord. I'll spare you the legal stuff, but the short version is he was planning to raise our rent by more than half when our lease expired in the fall. There was no way we could afford to pay the extra, so we were going to have to move again.

By the time we got our apartment, and me in Ponderosa High, we had moved more than twenty times. The first dozen or so were with my dad, after his meth habit got us evicted for not paying rent, or for some of the criminal stuff he was involved in. After that, we moved every time he found us. Coming north to Portland from Eugene was Mom's idea, getting far enough away that he wouldn't come after us. Between the distance and a long jail sentence, it had worked for almost six months. We'd been able to stay in the same place.

It was a personal record, and our landlord was going to take that away from us.

I had found friends at Ponderosa, a family of warriors I loved and respected, who took care of me and let me take care of them. I didn't want to move away from that, or even from our tiny apartment with its pretend dining room. I didn't want to. It wasn't fair.

But I could worry about that later. There was nothing for me to do right then, in the car surrounded by love, and excitement, and music that was great even if it was older than Mom, even older than Alex's car. I put it away, imagined writing the problem on a piece of paper and folding it up to put in my back pocket for later. The smile came back to my face. I joined my friends and Freddie Mercury singing about how nothing really matters.

As Alex took the last corner before we reached the parking lot for school, I spotted Susan Freaking Parker at the corner. She stood there with her brown hair blowing in the winter wind, wearing tight runner's leggings over her championship track star legs and under a bright red sweatshirt with the Nike swoosh in gold. She was staring out across the intersection.

"Guys, this is my stop," I said.

"Saw that coming," Galhardo said. He blew a raspberry. Sage and Fiel groaned, but Alex pulled the car over.

"Don't listen to them, *Chuugi*," She said. "Plenty of people abandon their friends to spend time with pretty members of the opposite sex. They're called losers." She let the car come to almost a complete stop before speeding up again. I did a little hop-skip we'd learned from Sensei and made it to the sidewalk almost gracefully.

Susan reached out with both arms and pulled me in for a kiss. It wasn't a smooch, but a real hello kiss, maybe deeper and longer than usual for us. That happened a lot whenever Susan and I were around Sage, but I tried not to think too hard about that. When she was finished, we turned and walked hand in hand down the sidewalk toward Ponderosa High School.

A little less than two months earlier, the school had been overrun with emotion-eating demons called *oni* under the direction of an elder *yokai* demon. They were growing powerful from the fear and anxiety of the teenage students, and working on some kind of plan. I had joined Fiel, Galhardo, Sage, and Alex in their fight against the demons and we drove them out. Well, most of them. And we never did find out about the plan the *yokai*, or the "master" it had mentioned, had.

But most of the demons were gone, thanks to us. I felt a little surge of pride as I saw how much happier and healthier the students around us looked now.

Susan poked my arm and said, "are you listening?"

"Huh? Sorry. I am now."

"I said, *big day today.*" Susan knew about the tournament, and was coming to watch as soon as she could get out of classes. She was a track star, and understood how important having her in the stands would be to me.

"Yeah," I agreed. My stomach agreed, too, rumbling around and fluttering as we walked.

"You've got this," Susan said.

"Yeah," I said again. My stomach butterflies weren't so sure.

"I mean, you had a good season. Even your leg seems okay."

"Yeah."

"You'll do fine."

"Yeah."

"Connor?"

"Yeah?"

"Your hair's on fire."

"Yeah...wait, what?" I stopped walking and looked at her.

Susan was laughing, her bright smile chasing away the nerves I'd been dwelling on. "Don't worry about it, Connor. Today's already all about you."

"Sorry," I said. "I'm just --"

She cut me off. "Your head's just already in the game. I get it. And I mean it: don't you dare worry about me. Just go make me a champion's girlfriend. Fair enough?" She leaned her head on my shoulder and we were quiet together until we got to her locker, where she stood straight and started fiddling with the lock. I felt a tap on my shoulder, and turned to see Tosha Mones.

Tosha was Susan's best friend, and somewhere between a frenemy and a nemesister for me. She was short, with black hair and brown skin. That morning, she had on a shapeless black dress that started low and ended high above boots that went up above her knees. She punched me gently on my chest, then opened her hand to stroke my stomach a little.

"Hey, studmuffin. Wanna see my new ink?"

"Isn't that illegal? Giving somebody a tattoo at our age?"

"That depends on where you get it, Sporty Spice."

"You didn't get it in Oregon?"

Tosha laughed. "Where are you from, again? The Shire?"

Over her shoulders, I saw Sage coming down the hall. It was time to head for the wrestling room and join the team. I kissed Susan goodbye, got a low five from Tosha, and moved through the stream of students to join my teammate.

I fell into stride next to her without slowing down. Behind us, Tosha said, "Mmmmm. Wrestlers. Which one has the nicer butt? Don't answer. I know what *you'll* say."

Sage held her fist out low for me to bump. I didn't know whether it was because of our nice butts, or for some other reason, but I bumped it as we kept walking. There's something about walking with a teammate toward a match that makes me feel like a complete badass, and I took a moment to enjoy it. Together, she and I had faced down demons, conquered evil, and scored the winning points in more than one wrestling meet.

My phone pinged as we rounded the corner by the locker rooms and wrestling gym. I slipped it out of my pocket to see a text message:

FIEL: Dad just called us in. We're golden. See you at the Rose Garden.

ALEX: Me, too. I'm driving.

GALHARDO: Palavra

FIEL: That means "word", Connor.

I texted back a smiley emoji, then put my phone away in time for Sage and I to walk into the wrestling gym together.

It felt empty. At a regular practice, more than forty of us filled the mat-floored room, moving around each other as we practiced, exercised, and drilled. Today, it held just the ten of us who had qualified for the state tournament, plus a handful of others who'd gotten permission to miss school and watch. Still, it was full of energy. Every athlete in there was moving. Some were running light warm-up rounds. Others were jumping rope or stretching. Still others stood mostly still, focusing on something inside themselves, but still shifting and sliding, carving shapes in space with their wills. Sage and I dropped our bags off and stepped on the mat to join them.

Mario DuPree broke off from the stretch he was helping Jordan Walker with. He was our varsity heavyweight, shorter than me but thicker and with a wider mean streak. I'd taken his slot when I'd arrived at Ponderosa the previous November, but he'd stepped back into it when I took a few weeks off to let my ankle heal. He had been the first demon-possessed person I'd ever had to fight, but he didn't remember that. He *did* remember how I'd cold-cocked him on the bus ramp after he started a rumor about Susan having cheated on me with him. I got a different kind of nervous as he walked up to us, limping a little in the strut he always used, but he smiled and offered me his hand to shake.

"You and me, Morgan. We ain't friends," he said, keeping his eyes on mine ." But it's us for gold and silver, deal?"

"Deal," I said. I took his hand and slapped his shoulder. "We'll see who's who on Saturday night."

"Oh, it'll be me." He let me go as Sage gave him a friendly shove. He shoved her back, but not so hard that I couldn't tell she scared him a little. Sage is smaller than both of us, but a black belt martial artist and the daughter of a Marine staff sergeant. The only smart people who aren't scared of her a little are the ones who are scared of her *a lot*.

Coach Russel came in through the athletics office doors then, accompanied by a hulking man with buzz-cut black hair and bulging muscles under a UFC t-shirt. Everybody ran to get in line. The ten qualifiers got into position in weight order, smallest to biggest, which put me at the end of the line. After me came a handful of spectators, all of us standing as close to attention as we knew how. Both men walked up and down the line, looking us over.

I knew Coach Russel, and was pretty sure the new man was named Mr. Waldron, a substitute PE teacher who'd been at Ponderosa since Mrs. Iko got hurt in a car accident. He didn't teach my classes, but I'd seen him and heard he was all right if you worked hard.

Coach opened his mouth to speak, but Mr. Waldron stepped forward and started talking. "Hello, lads! I'm here to wish you luck today. Some of you are going to wrestle just in high school. The rest of you will make it to college, maybe even the Olympics. But there's nothing after that. This isn't basketball or football."

He paused for a minute to let what he said sink in. None of us would disrespect Coach Russel by being rude to him, but I could tell by how my teammates shifted around that they were confused by this weird pep talk.

"But there is the UFC. That's a real career, make you rich and famous, and they love wrestlers. Randy Couture, and Brock Lesner, and Sara McMann were all wrestlers. So if you get a chance, come by my gym. I train MMA fighters when I'm not here teaching badminton." He smiled like he thought that was funny.

Coach cut in. " Do you know who else was a wrestler? Neil deGrasse Tyson, Robin Williams, and Maynerd from Tool. But feel free to check his gym out when the season's over. It can be good cross-training." He paused for a long moment, then shouted. "To business. Are you ready, gentlemen?"

We all shouted *Oooah! Oooah!* like in that movie *300*, which was coach's favorite film. All of us except Sage. She waited until we were done, then she shouted "I'm not a man, coach! And I ain't gentle!"

We laughed. It was a ritual we'd done all year, even Sage's part, and it made us all feel stronger. Coach gave the line one more pass.

"Scholars and warriors, every single one! Let's do this!"

We cheered again, then grabbed our bags and jogged single-file to the bus waiting outside.

CHAPTER 4

Heavyweights wrestle last in Oregon, so it was almost eleven in the morning before I had my first match. I got to the mat just as DuPree walked off, the opponent he'd just beaten 13-1 slinking away on the opposite side.

I held out a hand for him to slap, which he did. "Kick his ass, Moana," he growled. It always felt racist when he said stuff like that about my Māori heritage, but less racist than some stuff I'd dealt with. Besides, I think he meant it to be nice even if it wasn't. Sometimes, intent is more important. So is choosing when and when not to respond to aggression. Right now, my energy needed a different focus.

I walked onto the mat feeling calm and ready. I'd checked the brackets while the 136 pounders were still wrestling, and knew my opponent was a guy I'd beaten by ten points the week before Christmas. Coach was busy with a match that would be a closer call, so Sage sat in the coach chair at our corner. My opponent, Kyle Singh from Gresham, shook my hand. Then the ref blew his whistle and my tournament started for real.

I surged forward, faked left, faked low, then came up hard inside of Singh's reach. I put my back against his chest and tucked my hip in with a move I'd borrowed from judo we practiced at the dojo. The throw lifted Singh's feet and knees above my head and I strained my shoulders to keep his landing soft. We hit the ground and I put on the pressure. The ref slapped the mat and the clock stopped at 1 minute, 14 seconds. Nowhere near fast enough to beat any records.

"Darn," I said. I got to my feet, then helped Singh up. We both went to the center. We shook hands, then the ref lifted mine into the air. As Singh walked off, I felt a change in the air. I *looked* at him.

Looking is a skill Bushido Warriors learn, a way of perceiving forces invisible to most people. It's one of the benefits of being part of a secret war against demons old enough to remember when humans were still afraid of fire. When you *look* at the world, you can see supernatural forces, including demons. *Oni* feed on negative emotions the way leeches feed on blood. There are a few around most of the time. Usually they're harmless without a more powerful demon to organize and control them. They're stupid, and selfish.

And one was on Singh's shoulder, probably enjoying the taste of his disappointment. There wasn't much I could do about it, but it was good to keep an eye on what was happening. I turned my attention back to the coach corner and walked up to Sage, who high-fived me with one hand and slapped my butt with the other. Behind her, Dupree gave me a thumbs up that he turned into a different hand gesture I won't describe.

I was about to return the favor when my Mom popped out of the crowd. She had on her medical scrubs, with a big EMT bag slung over one shoulder and her hair under a blue ball cap that said MEDIC in white letters. She smiled and said, "Congratulations, Tiger. Can I hug you?"

"Only if you can make me look really tough while you do it."

"No promises," she put her arms around my waist and her face against my chest. I squeezed her back and the joy radiating off of us literally knocked the *oni* off of Singh from fifty feet away. That's their weakness. Negative emotions feed them, but positive feelings like love, or joy, or hope, burn them and make them weak. They run away from it as fast as their nasty little legs, or wings, or whatever will carry them.

I pulled away from mom and looked at her. "I read the letter."

She frowned, but made herself relax. "I said you could." She sighed.

"It sucks," I said.

"Yeah. It does. Have you come up with any brilliant solutions?"

"I've...sort of been busy...with the tournament."

"Don't worry, kiddo," Mom said. She put a smile back on her face. "We'll think of something. You need to stay here, near your friends."

As if on cue, the loudspeaker called out Sage's name for her next match. I saw her jog behind Mom, and raised a fist I was pretty sure she didn't notice. Mom gave my arm a squeeze. Her hand barely fit halfway around anymore. "Go. She'll want you to cheer for her."

I hugged Mom goodbye, and worked my way through the crowd toward Sage's mat. Even though they only allow athletes, coaches, officials, and press on the actual floor during the tournament, it's still crowded. I went as fast as I could but still almost missed it. Over the heads of another line of crowd, I saw a pair of heels move in an arc. I heard a hand slap the mat as a whistle blew.

By the time I got to the mat, Sage was already standing with her hand held in the air. I looked at the timer and saw seven-point-one seconds: a new tournament record for women. As her opponent retreated toward her coach, I *looked* and saw she had no demons on her. She was just naturally and appropriately disappointed.

But then I *looked* up and around. I'd forgotten to do that with my opponent, distracted by getting congratulations from Sage, Mario, and Mom. But now I looked up into the crowd to see thick flocks of the demons roosting in the rafters. They nearly obscured the big score board the Trailblazers used for their home games, and they packed the shadowy corners of the roof like...uh, well, like dozens of demons crammed into a small, dark space.

Sage broke my concentration and the vision faded, replaced by her pumping fist and fierce smile.

"Sage!" I said.

"Yeah, Connor! Yeah! Feels good. Damn good, doesn't it?"

"Yeah, I know. But."

"Tournament record, baby!"

"Yeah. That's great. You're a monster. But..."

"But what? But me no buts, boy, lest yours be the next one I kick."

"No. For serious."

"What?" Sage's smile fell. The urgency in my voice had finally penetrated her excitement.

"*Look*!"

"Look at what?"

"No, *look*." I pointed at the rafters and corners, up in the ceiling.

Sage shut her eyes and breathed into her belly. She had taught me how to *look* not long ago, when I first learned what the mark on my shoulder meant and joined the Bushido Warriors in their fight against the forces of evil. When her eyes opened, the smile dropped off her face, replaced by a grimace of worry. Then her mouth closed in a thin line of resolve. Sage wasn't the bravest person I knew, but only because I honestly wasn't sure she thought failure was possible. She's never really afraid, and being afraid is the first step in being courageous.

"Woah," she finally said.

"Yeah, woah."

"What does it mean?"

"I was hoping you could tell me."

CHAPTER 5

Wrestlers who win their first match get just one more on Thursday, so Sage was already done. I would have some time before my second bout, so we checked out with Coach Russell and headed toward the stadium seats. Susan was up there, waiting for me, along with Fiel, Galhardo, and Alex. I'd seen them holding a sign that said VOTE CONNOR FOR CHAMPION earlier that morning, and they'd spread enough stuff out on the seats around them to save room for both of us.

Susan didn't know about the Bushido Warriors. She just thought we trained together at a regular karate school that didn't have a whole lot of students. Fiel, Galhardo, and Alex were fellow Warriors, though. Each of us had a different mark on our bodies, a mark in the shape of a Japanese symbol. Mine stood for *Chuugi*: Loyalty. Sage's stood for discernment, Fiel's for Honor, Galhardo's for Bravery, and Alex's for Compassion.

The story goes that a warrior is born for each of the seven principles of the Bushido Code: honor (*meiyo*), courage (*yuuki*), compassion (*jin*), duty (*gi*), and loyalty (*chuugi*). Those warriors find each other every generation, and are bound together to fight *oni* and the demons that control them. We hadn't yet met *makoto* (truth) or *rei* (courtesy), but our Sensei said we should expect them soon.

All seven warriors only found one another when a threat was truly dire. That so many of us were together at this time had us all worried, but there wasn't much to do about that just now. Except to point out to my companions how *oni* were flooding the place.

As we neared the exit from the colosseum floor, I saw Galhardo's head in the crowd down there with us. We steered toward him, and saw Fiel and Alex. Susan was there too, and she squeezed through the crowd to hug me.

"You're sweaty! Ewww!" she said. But she didn't let go as she kissed me after. "Baby, that was a great pin. I'm so proud of you." She looked past me to Sage. "You too, gorgeous."

"Aw shucks," Sage said. "That was nothing. I saw you in the 200 hurdles finals last year. I'm just trying to live up to your example, girlfriend."

"Pshaw," Susan said. She stopped hugging me, but gripped my hand tight in both of hers. They stared at each other, something happening between them that I didn't really understand.

After a while, Sage smiled brightly and said, "How are you guys down here?"

Fiel smiled and lifted a plastic lanyard hanging from his neck. It had the word **PRESS** vertically along one edge, and the words *Wrestling 101 Podcast* at the center.

"What?" I said.

Sage said, "You forged press passes?"

"I'm a blogger," Galhardo said. "They should have given me one. It was obviously an oversight."

"Me, too," Susan said. She let one of her hands let go of me, and produced a lanyard saying she was with OregonTeenSports.com. Fiel and Alex also had press passes, and nobody seemed to be stopping any of them. We moved together off the main floor and into the service hallway. It connected to the food vendors. I could smell the hot dogs and nacho almost-cheese.

"Did you see Sage's match?" I asked everybody.

They all cheered and hooted for her, and Sage smiled remembering her victory. We would mostly tease her about it, but she really did have a chance at making the women's Olympic wrestling team sometime during or after college. If our war didn't have other plans for her.

Fiel said, "What a *match* it was, you really *lit* her up."

Galhardo looked at him and made a quiet golf clap while everybody else groaned. He waggled his eyebrows and pointed to Sage. "She really is *on fire* today."

Susan said, "I was scared for Sage at first. I thought her opponent would *come bust* her up." Everybody cheered, and Galhardo's eyebrows shot up in surprised approval. He held out a fist for my gal to bump.

Sage put her arm around Susan's shoulders and pulled her away from me, announcing, "I didn't come all this way to play second *char*."

"Honestly, you *smoked* her," Alex rattled off in a monotone with hardly any space between the words. "You truly embar*rassed* her. Kicked her *ash*. Brought the *heat*. You'd be rich if she had to pay you for how much you outclassed her at just a *cent-a-grade*. Also, something about Kelvin."

I said, "Yeah, Sage. Her performance really wasn't that *hot*."

Everybody grew silent, quiet enough we could hear the hum from the ice machine in a kitchen somewhere down the corridor. Galhardo gave me a dirty look. "Fine. Be that way. I have to pee." I kissed Susan on the cheek and wandered through the halls to the locker rooms.

I'd seen them before during weigh-ins, but every time I walked into the changing rooms at the Moda Center I was always struck with how much nicer they were than the ones at Ponderosa. Not even the rich high schools out in West Linn or North Beaverton had locker rooms like these. They were made for teams competing in front of crowds of tens of thousands of people, with soft carpet underfoot and benches made of real wood. They were also huge, so it took me a little while to find the actual toilets.

I looked down each row between locker banks, looking for a telltale flash of porcelain or a door leading to another chamber. They were all empty, except for one with an old man in a long trench coat sitting down playing with his phone. There was something familiar about him, but I had other priorities. I'd just about given up when I spotted Singh, my opponent from that morning, come out from a corner I'd thought just had a wall. I walked toward him and saw a doorway behind him. As we passed, I said "Hey" and offered a low five. He skittered away from me like I was contagious.

"Hoookay, then," I said to myself. But I had something more urgent on my mind. I walked through the doorway into a tiled room with toilet stalls on one side and a bank of showers on the other. I turned right and reached to take the straps down for my singlet.

CHAPTER 6

I almost had my singlet down when I heard my name come over the PA system.

"Calling Connor Morgan and Dale Cloud to Mat 8. Connor Morgan of Ponderosa High and Dale Cloud of Hillsboro High School to Mat 8."

Nerves flooded my system, starting at the backs of my legs and rolling up through my stomach to my ears. Cloud was a beast, a senior already getting a football scholarship to Notre Dame. He wrestled to get better at picking people up and throwing them back down again.

I pulled my straps up, turned around, and ran back to the floor.

I got to the mat and Sage was there, walking toward Mat 8 with Susan right behind her. Susan put her hand on my back and said, "Good luck."

Sage said, "Cloud is a mountain."

"You're telling me."

"You can still beat him," Susan said. "Right?"

"Maybe," Sage said. We stepped over the separation tape where Susan's press pass did no good. I turned around and mouthed *sorry* to her. She blew me a kiss.

I turned around and almost tripped when I saw Cloud. He stood there, on the other side of the mat, as tall as me and thicker in the chest. When he turned toward his coach, I could see zits on his back that told me he used steroids.

"Okay," Sage said after giving a low whistle. "Here's what you're going to do."

"Get my face broken off?" Out on the mat, two boys about Sage's size were trying to throw one another. I didn't know either of them, but I could tell they were tired. It was already the second round, and they were lumbering slowly in their fatigue.

Sage said, "He's a 'roid monkey and an aggro fighter. Use the *aikido* Galhardo works on us in practice. Make him break his own face."

"Yeah," I said. "Okay. That." At our dojo, Sensei had each of us take turns teaching our specialties to one another. I taught wrestling. Sage taught a Chinese martial art called kenpo. Alex taught kung-fu. Fiel taught us a martial art from his parents' home country of Brazil, called *capoeira*.

Galhardo was only a little bit more than half of my size, and had only three-quarters of a functioning body. His specialty was *aikido*, a Japanese martial art that uses an attacker's strength against them. He could capture my energy and throw me as if I were the smaller one. It was about timing, and fluid movement, and Sage was right. If I used those principles, and got it right, I could make Cloud do exactly what I wanted.

If I got it right. And if I survived the times I got it wrong.

Coach Russell came up then, breathing heavy from having run after somebody else's match. He put a hand on my shoulder and caught my eyes. "Tough draw, Connor. But here's what you're going to do. Wait for him to come at you hard, which he'll do, then use that to make him fall on his face." Sage winked at me from across his shoulder. "Don't worry. You've got this."

I snapped on my headgear and warmed up while the match played out in front of me. It went the distance, all three rounds, giving me just enough time to focus on worrying about what Cloud would do to me. If I won, I'd wrestle on Friday no matter what. If I lost, I'd have to win my third match of the day, or that would be it for me. So really, all I had to do was to not die.

The other match ended, 4-2 with points that must have been scored before I got there. The ref called us out. We shook hands, and got to work.

Cloud came at me hard with a double-leg takedown that was too strong for me to fight. We hit the mat like two trees falling, and the first thing I thought of was how I'd forgotten to pee. The impact made my bladder flare like fireworks and I groaned. Only after it receded did I register that I was on the ground, and Cloud had just scored two points.

Then Cloud was off of me. He stood up, letting me go. Wrestlers who are better at takedowns than at ground wrestling do that sometimes, allowing the point for an escape so they can take an opponent down again. But Cloud wasn't usually a takedown wrestler. He liked leg rides and arm bars and other moves that hurt, but he was letting me up.

I didn't understand, but I got to my feet. The ref called my escape point, making the score 1-2. Only when I saw Cloud's face did I get it. He'd seen how the takedown hurt me, and wanted to do it again. Which he did right there, barreling into me with something between a takedown and a football tackle. We hit the ground and I almost screamed. Then he let me back up.

He barely gave me time to stand before he hit me again, making my insides shiver and scoring another two points. Cloud didn't let up with that punishment until the whistle blew and he'd done it seven times. The round ended with him leading, 14-7, and me pushing back tears from the pain in my middle.

The second the buzzer sounded, Coach Russell started shouting at the other coach, and at the ref. He let them, and most of the Portland Metro Area, know Cloud was hitting too hard. The having to pee thing was my own problem, but Coach probably had a point. I could hardly breathe from the pain.

I forced myself to stand upright, and to put my hands behind my head and stretch the muscles in my belly and back. I breathed, filling my lungs, and imagined the pain as a bright red ball in my belly. With each breath, I made the ball get smaller until the pain was a tiny thing I could control. Then I opened my eyes.

Mom was right there, looking worried. I winked at her and gave a thumbs-up. Then I looked past her to Susan and my friends. They were all staring with round O shapes on their mouths. Susan might have been crying.

The ref cautioned Coach, who was still shouting, and Coach shut up. I turned around and jogged to the center of the mat. My insides were still a bundle of cramps, but I had it in its proper perspective. It was no longer bigger than me.

Cloud was already at the center, smiling with anticipation. He won the coin toss. Coach and Sage groaned as Cloud chose both up.

I winced, but took my position. I knew Cloud's game now, could work with it now that I was only hurt instead of hurt and afraid. He was looking forward to dishing out more pain. If that made him careless, I could get him to overextend and use Galhardo's aikido techniques and ruin his day.

He was too fast off the whistle, and took me down again. My game plan crumbled from the next wave of pain, and he jumped off of me almost immediately. I rolled to my feet, making it wide to give myself extra distance, but he hit me again. I got half a sprawl out, and he threw me sideways into the scoring table. Our combined weight knocked it over and sent the scorekeepers scrambling out of the way.

The ref called a time-out while they reassembled things. I stood with my back to the mat, Coach saying words I wasn't really understanding. I had never needed to pee so badly, and my back hurt from hitting the table. When we got called back to the center, I saw the score was at 8-16.

I staggered to the center again, my stomach cramping so badly I could barely stand. The red ball was gone, leaving only bright lines of agony everywhere. I breathed deep, dug deeper, and shifted my weight forward onto my toes. It wasn't enough for Cloud to see, but it would give me an extra quarter-second when he came at me.

Which he did, hard and fast as the whistle blew. I shot my legs backward and landed with my chest on the back of his head and neck. I hit him hard with a cross-face, twisting his head around until he was up on his toes. I stepped in for the same hip throw I'd put to Singh earlier, but Cloud was a better wrestler than that. He pushed into me, adjusted his legs, and shut the throw down.

I had been expecting that, hoping for it. Cloud always met force with force. He expected to be met the same way.

Instead, I turned my wrestling hip throw into an aikido osatugiri. Blending with Cloud's strength, I pivoted around our center. He went over, and hit the mat with the combined power of all 470 of our pounds. It shook the table when we landed, and my friends cheered louder even than the slam of our bodies. I rolled to face him, my chest on his chest and only my toes touching the ground.

The ref counted off my takedown and near fall points, adding five to my score for a total of 13-16. I'd closed the margin, but not by enough. I bore down hard, but he kept scrambling to keep one shoulder off the mat, and then the other.

"Short time!" his coach yelled from the sideline. "Short time, Cloud!"

I shoved my shoulder into the hollow between his head and neck, driving there with as much of my weight as I could. I scooped up one leg, but he still used the other to keep himself mobile. I was running out of time.

"Scoop the other leg!" Coach shouted.

I heard Fiel's voice over the crowd, "Kill him, Legolas! Bring him down!"

Cloud muttered something that rhymed with something rude. He bucked hard, but I took the opportunity to scoop up his other leg. That took away his ability to move, and I bore down on his chest with everything I had in me.

"Move, Cloud! Movemovemove!" his coach shouted. But it was too late. The ref slapped the mat and my side of the mat erupted into deafening cheers.

Cloud didn't even come to shake my hand. He stomped off the mat, throwing his headgear into the crowd. I let the ref hold my hand up for half a second, then I ran for the restrooms.

CHAPTER 7

I slapped Susan's hand on the run and sped through the crowd back toward the locker rooms. She gave me a hurt look, but Sage said, "He probably has to puke. Wrestling Cloud is like fighting a roller-coaster."

Fiel asked, "Can a roller-coaster be an asshole?"

The cramps made every step agony, which felt unfair. My body needed to pee worse than it ever had, but the way it told me so delayed my ability to let it pee. I seriously worried I would wet myself like a kindergartener, but I made it to the locker rooms one painful step at a time.

I peeled off the straps of my singlet as I shuffled past an old man. He was done fiddling with his phone, and instead just leaning against a locker looking as sketchy as...well, um, an old man hanging out in the locker room at a high school sports thing. I guessed he was either a janitor, or some kind of a creeper. If he was a janitor, that was fine. He was probably there to keep us kids from messing up the super-fancy locker rooms. If he was a creeper, he could go right ahead and creep on me. I was fifty pounds heavier, a varsity wrestler, and a soldier in an ancient, supernatural war.

They call that *natural consequences*.

But first I had to pee. I half-ran, half-limped between the lockers and into the tiled room with the showers and toilets. My stomach and hips felt like they were on fire before I was able to struggle out of my singlet and let the first drops fall.

"Bwaaaaaaa!" I groaned when the pressure finally released. If you've ever peed after really having to go for a long time, you know how good it feels. If you haven't, it can't be explained. The only thing better is doing it off of someplace high like a bridge, or a cliff.

I just let myself feel the release, letting my victory over Cloud sink in while the pain subsided, feeling the aches and pains in other parts of my body. He had worked me over, and my ankle was starting to rebel a little over the punishment I'd been putting it through. While I was doing my physical inventory, I heard somebody coming up behind me. I shifted slightly so I could see the reflection in the steel of the plumbing above my urinal.

It was the old guy. Even though the reflection was warped and cloudy, I could tell from the trench coat and the swatch of grey hair. It was him, and he was watching me pee.

Definitely a creeper, I thought to myself.

"Or maybe somebody possessed by an *oni*," the creeper said.

"Yeah, maybe." I said, relaxing a little before I tripped to the weirdness. My stream stopped and I yanked on my singlet straps. "Wait, what?"

"Connor Morgan," the creeper said. He was close, but just out of reach for an elbow or rear kick. "Remember that time we marched at an equal rights protest and you kept stepping in horse droppings, and Fiel and Galhardo stepped in them too because you were so embarrassed?"

"Uh...no?"

The creeper slapped his forehead. His voice was higher and smoother than I would have expected. "Right...remember that time you carried me off my front lawn after demons almost killed me, and then we got pulled over on the way to the hospital and a cop almost shot you?"

My head spun with confusion and fear, even though the creeper kept his distance. I pulled my singlet all the way up and turned to face the old man. What he'd just said had happened. But it had happened with Alex, and Sage, and Fiel, and Galhardo. This guy was old enough to be Alex's grandfather's uncle, and he was a...uh, a guy.

I backed up until the cold urinal pressed against my legs, while I looked at the man in front of me. He was short and thin, but looked strong. Despite his age, there was a youthful energy in his eyes and face that I swore was trying not to break into a smile. Not only that, there was something else...

And then it happened.

That vague sense of familiarity snapped into recognition. He looked like Alex, so much so that he could actually be my friend's grandfather's uncle.

"Are you related to Alex Haber?" I asked. It made sense. If he was Alex's family, she might have trusted him with that secret. He would tell me why he was standing guard in the locker room, and then everything would start to make sense.

"Guess again," he said. His face broke into a smile I recognized as he let his trench coat fall open. Then he made a tiny gesture with one hand and shifted. Her shape didn't change, but something did. The shape of her neck and shoulders, the movement in her face, the drape of her hair suddenly became feminine.

When I gasped in surprise, the woman in front of me smiled in a way I recognized. She turned her head until I could see the mark on the back of her neck: two lines on top of each other next to something like a sloped letter T.

I had the same kind of mark on my back, but hers stood for *Jin*, compassion. Only my friend Alex had that mark. Only my friend Alex could have that mark...and then I saw my friend. Her face was there in front of me, hidden under decades of age, work, sadness, joy, and hardship. Under it all, the herness, the *Alexness* shone through. This was my friend, just somehow seventy years older.

"Alex?" I said, slowly, while my brain caught up with my mouth. "But...what? What...happened? And why are you in the men's locker room? And why are you watching me pee!?!" That last part absolutely did not come out in a high, squeaky voice even though my female friend watching me pee was somehow weirder than the thought of some creeper doing the same thing.

Alex put her coat back in order and reached out to me with one hand. She smiled again, looking into my eyes, and said, "Get out of the John, Connor. Come with me if you want to live."

CHAPTER 8

"Wait, what?" I said again.

The old woman gave her most Alex-like expression yet, the one that showed she was disappointed with something. And just like that, she was Alex in my mind. An older Alex with lots of extra mileage, but my friend no matter what she looked like at that moment.

"Alex," I said.

"Yes," she said. The disappointed look softened into a serene, amused calm. That expression looked more like Sensei than anybody else, but didn't make the woman in front of me anyone other than Alex Haber, *Jin*, my friend.

"What's going on?"

"I'm from the future, Connor."

I blinked. "Uh, I'm sorry. It...well, um, it sounded like you said you're from the future."

She waved her hands in a kind of spooky finger motion, and made her voice into a wavering ghost sound. "Froooom the fuuuuuuchuuuuure!"

"Come on," I said. "Time travel?" Really? Joke's over, Alex. "Who did your makeup? It was Fiel, wasn't it? And why are you in the men's room?"

"For serious, Connor. I'm from the future. Just roll with it, okay? This isn't even the weirdest thing I'm about to tell you."

"Oooookay," I said. I glanced around, looking for my warmups. Assuming Fiel and Galhardo hadn't gotten Alex in on their most elaborate joke ever, this felt like it would be the kind of conversation I would want to wear clothes for. But they were in my gym bag, which I'd left on the floor next to mat 7. "What was that about coming with you if you want to live?"

"Damn," Alex said. "I owe Sage a hundred bucks."

"What?" I said.

"They're 2112 bucks, but still."

"What are you saying, Alex?"

"We watched *Terminator* with you last month Connor. This last month. Like, three weeks ago."

"So?"

She blew out her breath in a frustrated raspberry. "Listen. We don't have much time."

"Doesn't time travel mean you always have all the time you ever need?"

"Maybe in bad books, but it doesn't work like that in real life."

"It doesn't?"

"When was life ever that easy?"

As if on cue, a hiss came from just outside the doorway into the locker rooms. Alex turned and I stepped up beside her, both of us *looking* in the direction of the noise. The shadows there, empty when I'd come in, were crawling with *oni*.

"Well now," Alex said. A thin smile played across her lips. "I always have time for that."

More *oni* than I could count slipped out of the shadows and stalked toward us. They were all small, about the size of basketballs, all in different monstrous forms. The least disturbing looked like a cross between a chihuahua and a scorpion.

"Okay, *Chuugi*," Alex said as she slid one foot backward into a relaxed fighting stance. I dropped my weight into a wrestling position, shuffling so I stood next to my friend. Or was it the woman my friend would one day become?

The monsters drew closer, spreading into a wide line to cut off our escape. They were three deep at the thinnest point. Alex stage-whispered out the side of her mouth, "You ready for a twenty-seven?"

"Awhatnow?"

"Right. We haven't come up with those yet. When they get to the doorway, run in front of me and attack from my opposite side. It confuses them"

"When they come at us?"

"When they come at us."

"Okay," I said. When I wasn't looking at the woman, she felt so much like my younger friend. She had the same movements, the same voice, the same *self*. Only with more experience, and a sense of much more power. I repeated, "When they come at us."

And then they came at us.

I still wasn't sure what a twenty-seven really was, but it worked pretty well.

When the front line of demons had to press together between ranks of lockers, I ran across and in front of Alex. It froze them for a second, all of their creepy eyes following my motion. I reached the opposite side and grabbed two oni that looked like praying mantises, pulling both into a rising knee strike that popped them like evil balloons. They vanished in curls of rank, greasy smoke. Alex charged into the middle while they were still motionless. By the time they recovered and began to fight back, we had shredded half their line and thrown the rest into panicked chaos.

Alex and I worked together, her responding smoothly to my motion as if she'd had decades of practice. The *oni* tried to swarm us, but whenever they came close to overwhelming one of us, the other was there to pick off demons while their backs were turned.

The fight was over before it had really begun, but there was something strange about it besides how well Alex coordinated with me. Something about how the *oni* moved, or was it the way they felt? Whatever it was, it was off. That didn't stop me from fighting them with all I had, though. Fighting demons is what I do.

Alex burst our final attacker, a snake-shadow with a head like a rooster, by kicking it into the corner of a bench. As its smoke rose to the ceiling, she raised her hands over her head to breathe in short pants. Once she caught her breath, she said, "Now, that wasn't so bad, was it?"

"No," I said. I wasn't out of breath, but then again I wasn't old yet. "No. But it was different."

"That follows," she gasped. "They're from the future, too. Must have followed me. The fight there. It's different. It's not easier. It's not harder, either. It's just...different."

"How?"

"I could tell you, *Chuugi*, but then I'd have to kill you?"

"Really?" I laughed. I assumed she was kidding, mostly. All the time travel movies I'd ever seen told me things could get weird when you went into the past.

"No. But telling you could actually kill you all by itself."

"Wait, really? I mean, really, really?"

Alex's face broke into the wide smile I'd known for months. "Yes. Maybe? I don't know. It's weird. And it's not well-understood. But here's what I *can* tell you."

"Okay. Yeah?"

"We're already traveling in time. The two of us. Right now."

"What?" I shouted. An electric shock of panic shot through me. Had I missed any matches? Was Mom worried about me? "Wait! I didn't say I wanted to!"

"We have no choice, old friend. We're both traveling, right now. Forward. Into the future."

"What do you mean? Where are you taking me?" My voice trembled a little as I asked the question I didn't really want an answer to. "How fast?"

"At a rate of exactly one minute for every sixty seconds."

"But that's not fair!" I shouted. "Today's important! If I miss my matches, my scholarship...oh. Wait."

"There he is," Alex said. She smiled again, that calm and happy smile that reminded me more of Sensei than the Alex I knew. "It sometimes takes you a minute, but you always get there. Certain things never change."

"So," I said. "Are we traveling in time right now, or not?

She sighed and patted my shoulder, that serene, amused look still on her face. "Here's what I really can tell you. Some of the rest I don't know. Some of the rest I don't understand. And some of what's left, I honestly couldn't tell you if I did know it, and understood it perfectly."

"Why not?" I asked.

"It's strange. Time is like a river, flowing in one direction. We're all swimmers, or boats, or leaves, or whatever else floating along in its big current. That's how it all works. Are you with me so far?"

I was surprised to find I thought I was. I nodded.

"If something big enough falls into the river, it makes ripples like when you drop a rock into the water. Time magic can enter the river in those ripples, including the ones moving against the flow."

"Okay."

"Nobody has ever been able to use magic to make that big thing fall, not that we know of. So the chances to see time magic in action are rare. It's not studied much, and understood even less. Believe me, if this was a thing we could just *do*, there are things I would change first."

"What? What would you change?"

"I'd tell you, but..."

"Okay. I get it. But why are you here?"

"I rode one of those ripples back in time to here, and we are riding another one further back."

"Why me? And why just me? Shouldn't we get Sage, and Fiel? What about Galhardo?"

"I can answer some of that, but we're in a hurry. I'll tell you once we get to the other side. I need you, and only you, and it can only be you. I know I don't really have to ask this, *Chuugi*, but are you in?"

I was confused, and a little scared, and a lot cold standing there in just my wrestling singlet. But Connor means "loyalty" in Old Irish, and *Chuugi* means the same thing in Japanese. I am the warrior of loyalty, and my friend was asking for my help.

I looked at the aged face in front of me, seeing my friend behind the lines, grey hair, and careworn brow. She smiled, because she could see my answer before I said it.

"I'm in."

CHAPTER 9

Alex said she couldn't risk being seen by her now-self, so I went to the floor to retrieve my bag and warmups alone. She told me to meet her by a door not far from the locker room entries in less than ten minutes.

"But it's time travel. Can't we leave whenever we're ready?"

"No. The ripples come when they come. It's like catching a loop pod."

"A what?"

She shook her head, laughing at herself. "A bus, Connor. It's a lot like catching the bus. Once it's gone, you've missed it. So ten minutes. Not fifteen. Not ten and a half."

"Okay."

Getting my bag took longer than I'd expected. It wasn't at mat 7, but I saw it by Coach at mat 4. He wanted to talk about my match, which took a few minutes. By the time we'd finished, Mom had found me and wanted to make sure I was okay. By the time she was convinced, I had to sprint down the hallway to the door. Alex was there, pacing back and forth with a shadow of worry across her otherwise serene face. When she saw me, she pulled out the cell phone she had been fiddling with when I first noticed her in the locker room.

"I thought those would be smaller by the time we're all as old as you," I said as I came to a stop beside her.

"First," she said, not looking up from whatever she was doing with the screen. "They are smaller. Most of us have them on the inside."

"Like an implant?" I'd read some stuff online about that. They sounded almost as awesome as they were super-duper creepy.

"More like a pill. Besides," she swiped up on her phone and the door in front of us unlocked with a click of metal. "Does your cell phone do that?"

"No," I said. "No, it does not."

Alex pulled the door open and gestured for me to go through it. Inside was a wide boiler room, full of big metal boxes and silver ducts. It was crowded with equipment, but big enough Alex and I could come in and shut the door behind us.

"So," I said, after waiting a minute in the close, hot space. "Alex. What are we doing?"

"Remember how I said it took something big jumping into the river to make time travel possible?"

"Yeah. The splash sends ripples backward, right?"

"Right. In this case, the big thing is a nuclear explosion."

"What? Now?" My heart raced and I took two steps toward the door. I had to get Mom to safety, and warn Susan, and Sage, and the other warriors. There were so many people in Memorial Coliseum, here for the tournament. "What are we going to do?"

"No!" Alex said. She grabbed my arm, gently but with a soft strength I knew I wouldn't be able to resist. "No. The explosion is in 1945."

"In 1945? How does that? Why do we..."

"Time travel, *Chuugi*. Remember? It's a huge explosion and it's important historically. Culturally. Its ripples are enormous, and last for centuries."

My heart rate slowed down to something closer to normal. Mom and my friends were still in some kind of danger. Alex wouldn't have come back in time for something that wasn't important. But they weren't going to die in a nuclear attack in the next ten minutes. "Okay," I said. "Okay. But why here, and why now?"

"I honestly don't know. The Bushido Warriors have something to do with it, and there's another factor."

"What's that?"

"I'm pretty positive I can't tell you."

I groaned. "This is going to get old. I can already tell."

"Sorry, old friend. There's just no other way."

"Can you tell me why?"

Alex walked deeper into the boiler room, toward a door in the opposite wall. While we moved, she said,

"Remember that *yokai* you killed a couple of months ago."

Boy did I. Alex, and I, and the other Bushido Warriors had fought somebody we *thought* was possessed by a powerful demon mastermind, only to find out it had possessed somebody else entirely. I ended up fighting it by myself, which was why my leg was still messed up weeks later even after sessions of magical healing. I nodded.

"Remember how it said something about *The Master*?"

"Yeah. He said there were lots of bad guys working for him." I didn't mention how much sleep that had lost me. The *yokai was* tough, way tougher than me. I wouldn't have survived if I hadn't fought really dirty at the last possible second. The idea that he wasn't the boss monster scared me more than I liked to admit to myself, let alone say out loud.

"We know who he is, and this is part of that fight. We are winning, but if I told you things out of the sequence, it could endanger that. This isn't a science fiction novel. We don't get do-overs. Access to the time streams just adds dimensions of responsibility."

Sensei had taught us about zones of influence and responsibility. It's simple. If you can influence something, especially if you can harm it, you are responsible for it. Swing your hand like you're punching. Everything inside that arc is your responsibility, because you can reach it. Now, pick up a stick and swing it. You're responsible for a wide area now. If I understood Alex, we were now holding a stick that extended all over the world, and all over history.

We reached the door. She swiped on her phone thing again. It unlocked, but she didn't reach to open it. Instead, she looked me in the eye and said, "Are you ready?"

"Yeah," I nodded. I offered her my fist to bump.

She looked at me harder, her eyes searching in a way I'd only seen before in Sensei or Mom. After a moment, she said. "You're not ready."

"What do you mean? I was born ready. I was *conceived* ready."

"No. You're not ready."

"Why?"

"Because I wasn't ready." She opened the door to reveal another room.

I couldn't tell you what kind of room it was, or what else was in it besides a swirling, purple and orange disk. The disk was on its side, parallel to the walls, and the inside looked like a cross between a tornado and a fireworks show. It filled me with wonder, and dizziness, and fear, all at once, and it radiated a...well, um, a *wrongness*. It was the sort of wrong feeling you get when a part of your body isn't just hurt, but broken. Only the wrong thing was with reality itself.

This was a wound in reality, like a bullet hole, or a bite from a demon. Like what happened to my arm the time I tried to protect Mom when my dad got drunk and I had thought I was big enough. I tried to swallow, but my mouth and throat were too dry. The gate made a windy, weeping noise as it rotated. Far down in the center of the wound, I could see the stars of a night sky.

"Woah," I said.

"See?" Alex said. "I told you you weren't ready. But yes, I agree. Woah."

"Woah," I said again.

"Ready or not, though," Alex said. "The gate won't be here forever." As if to confirm what she said, the gate began to shift. The distant, starry field grew larger, seeming to come closer despite not moving at all. It made me seasick to see it.

"And we're going *inside* of that?" my voice squeaked the words out through a throat tight with fear.

"That's the plan."

"Is it going to hurt?"

"Not even a little bit. This will be like jumping into cold water. Better to just get it done."

I grabbed her hand. Like little kids, we ran to the gate and jumped toward those strange, near-but-distant stars.

CHAPTER 10

It took no time at all to pass through the gate. Almost before we jumped, I landed hard on something harder. I tried to roll it out, using the breakfall techniques I had learned at the dojo, but ended up just skidding across a rough and uneven surface. All my nerves sizzled like when you hit your elbow on the corner of a door. I was blind from it, struggling to breathe. When the pain receded enough for me to see, I realized I was on my back. Above me was a starry sky, partially covered with clouds. I turned my aching neck, fighting waves of dizziness, and saw Alex gasping on the ground nearby.

When I could talk, the first thing I said was, "You *butt*hole!"

Alex groaned. She rolled her head to look at me, her face half-covered with grey hair. "What?"

"You said it wouldn't hurt."

She sat up, smiled, and gave a coughing laugh. "One of your best friends tells you something crazy isn't going to hurt, and you just believe her? That, good sir, is on you."

She had a point. I breathed deep into my belly and let the clean air push out the last of the pain. I rolled over, pushed up to my hands and knees, and stood to look around.

We were up on a hillside, at night. The sky was full of stars, but no moon shone. Below us were the shadowed silhouettes of a city, with the darker line of a river snaking through it. Near where the river met a wide darkness, lights of some kind of factory blazed. I could hear the sound of machinery working from where we stood.

It took a while to realize what was wrong with the rest of the city. It was completely dark. No lights shone from any windows. No street lights lit the roads. The outlines of the buildings were odd, too, a different shape than the buildings I was used to.

"Alex," I whispered in the dark. "Where are we?"

"Nagasaki."

"Like, in Japan?"

"Exactly like that, Connor. We are in Nagasaki on the eighth of August, 1945."

That rang a bell, but I couldn't tell why right away. "Should I know that date?"

Alex reached for her smarter-than-a-smart-phone. "No. But you might know tomorrow."

"Um," I said. "Tomorrow like the day after the day you found me, or tomorrow here tomorrow?"

"After sunrise here, Connor," Alex said. There was a hint of frustration in her voice, making her sound like she was once again closer to our age. "You might know the date of August ninth, 1945."

"Why?"

"Where are we?"

"Nagasaki. You just said."

"Why do you know this place? That name?"

"I don't know. Give me a minute." As I thought, the air around us buzzed with the humming of some kind of insect, like a cricket with an amplifier.

Alex said, "What name do you associate with the city of Nagasaki, Japan?"

The answer came to me right away, though I couldn't yet say why. "Hiroshima."

"And why is that, *Chuugi*?" Despite her earlier impatience, Alex's voice was calm. It felt like one of Sensei's lessons where he would lead us to the truth by asking questions until we found our own answers.

I tried to do that. I thought about why I connected Nagasaki and Hiroshima in my mind. It was something important. Something from history class.

Then it hit me.

"Oh. Oh...hell, no."

"Hell, yes, as it turns out." Alex put her device away. "Okay. This is the earliest of four temporal ripples we could reach from your time. It's ten at night here. The atomic bomb called Fat Man falls at 11:02 tomorrow morning."

"What? Why?" I said. I wasn't panicking, even though we were less than a day away from one of the worst things to even happen in world history, and no distance from the place it happened. "Why are we here? What's happened...Alex, did you turn into a bad guy?"

She laughed. "No, Connor. If I were a bad guy, I would have killed you when you were still helpless from the time jump. I've done bad things, my friend. We've all done things we weren't proud of in the war against the demons. I've made mistakes. I've decided on things that weren't mistakes, but still got people hurt. But that's not the same thing as turning into a bad guy. At least I really hope not. Anyway, do you see those train tracks?"

It took a little while in the dark, but I finally spotted the parallel metal lines gleaming in the light from the factory, snaking past us at the bottom of the hill. Once I saw them, I could follow their path in a winding line past intact buildings, ruined houses, and holes where something used to be before a normal Allied bomb had hit.

Alex continued. "Sensei was supposed to leave on those tracks three hours ago. He was going north to help the survivors of the Hiroshima bombing. But the enemy rode a different time ripple, and they somehow kept him here."

I whispered her words to myself, repeating them until they made some kind of sense. A bad guy had gone back in time to try to kill Sensei before he could meet and train us. "So we're here to get him out of town?"

"Exactly." She pointed further into the city, where it began to rise up along the hills on the other side of the narrow river valley. "See that building right there? That's the dojo, in this place, at this time."

I followed her fingers with my eyes and saw the outline of a huge temple rising four stories above the buildings surrounding it. "That one? With the roof like something on a *National Geographic* special?"

"No, the one on the left, with the eaves half-destroyed."

I traced my eyes left and saw only a blank space between the temple and a house on a hill. Then I dropped my eyes a little to see a tiny shack, barely visible. It was so small next to the temple, and even next to the big house. It looked like nothing at all.

"That shack?"

"Yes."

"That shack. The one I can barely see, that looks small enough to be an outhouse for the people in the temple?"

"Yes," Alex said. I could hear the smile in her voice. It sounded like Alex from my time. "Are you surprised?"

I thought about that for a moment. "No. Not really."

"Okay. See that arch over there?"

I saw it immediately, standing starkly by a cluster of trees. "Yeah."

"The bomb explodes a few hundred feet from it."

It didn't take me two seconds to do the math about how close that was to Sensei and the dojo. I did not sound like a terrified teenager when I said, 'We need to get Sensei on the next train."

"Yes, *Chuugi*. Yes we do."

I nodded to myself, looking out over the dark city. So much of it was already in ruins. Factories surrounded by rubble, homes destroyed. Everybody there would be huddled in the dark, fearing another bombing run from an enemy they hadn't chosen and couldn't fight. Huge piles of debris sat where people probably used to live happy lives. And it would all be so much worse in less than a day.

"*Jin*," I said, using her warrior name. "Can we stop it?"

The smile vanished from my friend's voice. "No, *Chuugi*. I don't think anybody can. It's like a scar in time."

"But we can make sure Sensei survives, and can help?"

She slid closer to me in the dark, and set her small, strong hand on my shoulder. "Yes."

"Alex? *Jin*?"

"Yes, *Chuugi*?"

"Then why are we still standing here?"

CHAPTER 11

We walked together down the hill and through neighborhoods of mostly intact houses, with wooden walls and those curved tile roofs you think of when you think about houses in Japan. The night was quiet, without even dogs barking. The only sounds were buzzing insects and the occasional clank or bang echoing over the water from the factory. Not even one light shone in any of the windows.

As we got to the bottom of the hill and into the city itself, we passed more signs of damage from the war. Holes gaped in the walls of homes, and piles of rubble lay where buildings once stood. Here and there we skirted jumbles of burnt wood and shattered stone, where the city's people had started to put order to the chaos of conflict.

The wind picked up, carrying with it a heavy odor of pee, sweat, poop, and misery.

"Eww, what is that?" I said.

Alex's face wrinkled. That face was strange to me. It was full of lines, and spots, and scars, but still the face of my good friend. I could see the Alex from my time, my Alex's smiles and scowls, in the lines at the corners of this older woman's mouth and eyes. Her face was sadder, too. It drooped a little, like it was carrying weight the Alex of my time had not yet picked up.

She squinted. "That would be the POWs."

"POWs?"

"Prisoners of war. There were...there are...wow, verb tenses are hard when you travel in time. There's a camp for prisoners of war a little less than two kilometers from here. They're mostly Allied troops from Australia, and United States soldiers captured in the Philippines."

"And we can smell them from all the way over here?"

"It's more than a thousand men packed into a tiny space, in the summer, in the tropics, without running water or flushable toilets."

"Oh," I thought about that, then thought about what might happen to them in less than a day. "They're just two kilometers from here? Can we save them?"

"No," Alex said. "For one, it would make too big of a difference in the future. Bad things could happen. For two, what would happen if we released a thousand allied soldiers in this part of Japan?"

I thought about what I would do, and realized the answer immediately. "They'd fight."

"Right. And if the armed and better fed Japanese troops here didn't just kill them all, they'd come into the city looking for food and shelter. Which would work out poorly for them in a little less than twelve hours."

"Won't it work out poorly for them anyway?"

"No. The camp is over the next hill. It acts like a shield, diverting the energy of the bomb upward like a ski ramp. Very few POWs die from the blast."

"So there's nothing we can do?"

"We can rescue Sensei. That will have to-" she closed her mouth in the middle of the word and held up a hand next to her ear. I listened, and a second later I heard it. Footsteps approaching from down a narrow, cobblestoned street.

We slipped around the corner of the temple, tucking ourselves into a niche between a support column and the fancy frame of one of its doors. Alex closed her eyes tight and whispered words I couldn't make out. The shadows around us deepened until I could barely see the four men passing just a few feet away.

I say they were men, but only one was an adult. The other three were teenagers, maybe even tweens. The man towered over them, head and shoulders taller and monstrously thin. His uniform hung loose on his frame, and one sleeve was empty where his left arm should have been. It was folded in half and pinned squarely to his shoulder, neatly pressed like the rest of his clothes. He glared at the boys, barking short, angry orders if one fell out of line.

The smallest, no larger than one of Fiel and Galhardo's many young cousins, held a long pole with a lantern at the end. It was the only artificial light anywhere near us, and didn't come close to penetrating the thick shadows Alex had called to our hiding place.

Still, I held my breath as they marched past us. Even in the dim light, I could see the teens were hungry and exhausted. Twice, the older soldier slapped one for reasons I couldn't tell. There was something in the way he did it that told me he liked it. I felt hot anger grow in my stomach, and took half a step forward, but Alex silently put a hand on my chest.

We waited together, barely breathing, until the patrol rounded the corner. Alex stood first, and I followed her lead. As we crept back onto the street, I whispered, "They look...Alex, they look awful. And they're just kids."

"Yeah" she said. "By this time in the war, every Japanese man or teenaged boy with anything like an able body was...dammit, is...in China, or Korea, or an island in the Pacific. Anybody still here was either wounded at the front, or not able to do the regular army. The same was true for supplies. They were fueling their planes with pine resin by now, and those guards probably ate grass for lunch today."

My heart hurt for those kids, even for the bullying veteran commanding them. Only the smallest part of war was a glorious battle against the forces of evil, and even those parts sent ripples of misery forward through time for years after. We walked toward Sensei's dojo, Alex somehow picking a true path through the ruined city.

We walked past a jumbled wreck that had obviously once been a school building. "Wow. They really did a number on this place even before."

"Yes," Alex said.

"But they started the war, right?"

"Mostly," Alex said slowly, as we stepped off the streets and into a park that still had its tall trees intact. The leaves were gone, even in the middle of summer. I wondered if somebody had eaten them. "Mostly, yes. And they did terrible things in Korea and China."

"So you could say they deserve all of this."

Alex stopped. She turned to look at me, her face so much like Sensei's in that moment, so strong and sad. Like she'd been hearing every terrible secret in the whole world for years, without anybody to talk with about them. Mom sometimes looked sad like that sometimes when she thought I wasn't looking.

"I can't," she said, slowly, like she was figuring out what she felt while she was saying it. "You might say Emperor Hirohito deserves it. He's the one who started the war, and he's living in a nice palace and still eating nutritious food. He'll even stay in power after it's all over. But those kids on patrol? Whoever used to live in that house right there? Do they deserve what's happening?"

Two months earlier, when I had become part of the war against the demons, we'd had to beat our principal unconscious to release her from a pack of demons. They'd been possessing her for almost a year. The woman she had been didn't deserve the things we'd done to her. Wars of all kinds lead to people getting hurt who don't deserve it, and the people who deserved a little hurt feeling a lot more than they had coming. I couldn't even be sure if the Emperor who started it all deserved it on his own, or because a powerful demon was riding him, controlling his thoughts, growing fat on the misery he spread across half the world.

I had no words for what I was feeling, so I just nodded to my friend and walked further into the park. Somehow, the entire space hadn't felt the fall of a single bomb. Somehow, people were still taking care of it. The grass was cut short, the bushes trimmed neatly. There was no trash or rubble anywhere I could see.

When we reached the last line of trees, Alex held her hand up in a fist. We stopped, waiting in the shadows, and looked out into the street outside.

"There it is," Alex said. I saw it, a humble shack on short wooden posts next to the columns of a temple five times its size. A small, dark alley ran between the buildings. Just like the dojo in my place and time, this one had a tiny porch at the top of a short set of stairs. Just like the dojo in my place and time, a pair of lion-dog statues sat on the porch, one on either side of the door.

Seeing it, I felt a sense of homecoming even though I was as far from home as I had ever been. Some things don't change. I'd felt that familiarity on the wrestling mat at every new school, back when Mom and I still had to move every few months. I felt that at dinner with Mom, no matter how many different places and times we ate together. Even in the women's shelter where we first hid to get away from my dad, I felt that. And now, even so distant in time and space, I felt it with the dojo.

I stood up, and walked toward my home. Alex walked with me.

We were just twenty steps from the stairs when a voice came from the narrow space between the dojo and the temple. *"Tasukete! Derekaga tasukete kedasai!"* I didn't need to understand Japanese to know the voice was calling for help.

Or to recognize the voice. It was exactly like the one I heard almost every day at the dojo. Seventy years earlier, it hadn't changed or aged. I ran toward the noise, with Alex right behind me, but when we reached the alley's mouth, it was empty of anything but shadows.

"Wait, what?" I said. I felt Alex's back press against mine while she muttered a series of very bad words.

The shadows coalesced into fat demonic forms with round faces and huge feet. They slipped out from between the columns of the temple, and from under the eaves above. I *looked*, and saw more creeping through the street behind us.

We were very, very surrounded, and Sensei was not in the alley.

CHAPTER 12

"So," Alex said. I felt her drop her weight into a fighting crouch. "*Tanuki.*"

"*Tanu*-OOF!"

A *tanuki* dropped on me from above, landing on my head. Its weirdly soft feet crushed against my face. They filled my mouth and eyes and nostrils with stinking, furry flesh. I struggled to get it off of me, my lungs burning earlier than they should have. My blinded eyes exploded with bright spots from lack of oxygen.

"Gah!" I shouted, throwing the thing to the ground. Cool air filled my lungs. "It choked me with its feet!"

"Not its feet!" Alex shouted back. I caught another *tanuki* in the air before it could drop onto my face, and threw it at a cluster of others lurking in a corner. They tumbled like pins in a bowling alley, then scampered back up the alley walls. From behind me came the sweet sounds of my friend laying down some serious smack of her own.

"What?" I said. Another demon got past my defenses, leaping from one of the temple columns. Its feet gripped around my head and neck like soft, nasty Play-Doh.

"Little busy now," Alex grunted. "I'll tell you when you're older!"

While I struggled to tear the demon off my face, more hit me in my legs and chest. I fell hard, still focusing on trying to breathe. Short claws grabbed at my clothes and pressed against the skin beneath. I couldn't get a good hold on the demon, so I punched its weird, smelly foot with everything I had. It squealed in more pain than I expected, and curled up into a ball. I grabbed it like a basketball and threw it like a chest pass into the nearest wall. It burst into oily smoke. I snatched up another by its feet and it screamed while I spun to standing, and used it to beat down the other demons surrounding me. By the time it disappeared into its own puff of shadowy air, its pack had all retreated into the shadows.

I shuffled backward toward the sound of Alex's fight, looking around to see dozens more monsters on all sides. These weren't just the weird, big-footed *tanuki*, but *oni* of all kinds. Crow shapes, and badger shapes, and snakes, and spiders, and combinations of all four, filled the dark spaces. Two more *tanuki* dropped from the temple roof, their feet somehow spreading to form little parachute pouches. On one hand, the high ground gave them a good position. On the other, the slow fall told me exactly where both would be for a few precious, predictable seconds. I judged the timing and kicked one into the other, using a muay thai kick I'd learned from Sage. They both disappeared with a squeal and pop.

"Alex!" I shouted. "How are we doing?"

"Okay!" her voice was ragged, short of breath. "Watch those rooflines!"

That first airdrop of demons had told me that, and they were coming from the ground, too. Dozens more crowded in from all sides. Behind me Alex was tiring despite her power and experience. I shuffled further back until I could feel the warmth of her presence and the wind of her motion, and got ready for the next charge. The demons crested like a wave, ready to crash over us both and drown us in their numbers and their alien, reckless hate.

"Come on!" I shouted to the horde.

"That's the spirit!" snarled Alex.

"*Kyoskete*!" A voice echoed in the chaos of the fight.

"What?" I shouted. A suicidally brave demon came scrambling in toward me, and I punted it football-style back into the crowd. "English! I know we're in Japan, but I don't speak—"

"That wasn't me!" Alex shouted.

"Who, then?"

Alex hip-checked me, turning us so we were both sideways to the front of the alley. The mouth was blocked, filled by four figures, three small and one larger. The largest was missing an arm, and they all were aiming guns at us.

A surge of fear and adrenaline burned through me. No way could we win a fight against both groups. The *oni* from my side ran toward us, and I got ready to take as many with me as I could, but they ran around us and climbed up the soldiers. They flowed into their ears and nostrils, until there was nothing left visible but the guards. All four hunched for a moment, then straightened and raised their guns again.

The *tanuki* in the alley had not entered the guards. They chittered and laughed in high, squeaky voices and climbed back to perch on the eaves.

The oldest guard punched his one arm forward, gesturing with a pistol. "*Anata wa dare?*"

"What?" Alex and I shouted, almost at the same time.

"*Anata wa dare?*"

"I don't understand!" I shouted. Alex said, "*Wakarimasen!*"

One-arm's voice lowered, and somehow got more dangerous. "*Idoo shinai!*"

Alex raised her arms, palms toward the frightened boys and their sadistic leader. "*Matte!*"

"Wait!" I said, trying to keep my voice calm. It was hard to do when people with guns were shouting in a language I couldn't understand. I just had to trust Alex's command of the situation, and of Japanese.

The boys moved forward a step, their legs shaking with fear and confusion. We must have looked like demons to them. Alex was small, but ghostly white compared to anybody they would have seen in their lives. I looked vaguely Asian, but not Japanese, and at six feet and 230 pounds was literally twice their size. The *oni* possessing them would be amplifying that fear, telling them to be angry we were in their city, telling them what we would do to their friends, and their mothers, and their sisters and little brothers, if they didn't stop us permanently that instant.

Little fingers tightened on triggers. Bayonets thrust forward. One-arm snarled. I glanced behind us for an escape route, but it was a long run to the end of the alley, and a hard climb up to a pack of *tanuki* once we got there. We were in a shooting gallery, with the only exit blocked by frightened children with guns. They might not have wanted to kill us, but the demons riding them surely did.

The only good news was they would wait a moment. *Oni* eat emotions like the fear and hate those kids were feeling. They would want to snack on it first, greedily slurping it down before they had our pain and death for dessert.

Then I saw a shadow standing behind them, a figure that loomed tall and broad, huge in comparison to the boys and the wounded, malnourished man. He walked with power, and purpose, until he stood directly behind the soldiers and shouted, "*Kare o tebanasu!*"

A flash of light blasted through the alley, carrying a feeling like thunder would make if it was pressure instead of sound. It filled me with a raw, angry power that made me feel like I could take on the entire city's worth of demons all by myself.

The *oni* ran out of the soldiers, scampering across the ground, walls, and each other in their hurry to escape. The boys shook themselves and turned toward the looming figure, while One-arm stood rigidly to attention. I moved to attack them while they were distracted, but neither the stranger nor they looked like they were going to fight.

He said something fast in Japanese, and One-arm said something back. Whatever it was, it made the three boys laugh, and One-arm lowered his pistol.

"What are they saying?" I whispered to Alex.

"They're talking about a sumo match they saw...um...last night? Last week? Probably last week. My *nihon-go* was never great."

The conversation wrapped up in just a few minutes, with the tall stranger thanking One-arm, and the group of guards walking away back into the park. Then the stranger turned toward us.

He would have been big in Portland of my time, and must have seemed a giant to the people here. The black mane of his short-cropped hair came up to just below my nose, and he carried enough muscle on him that he might have outweighed me. His black kimono seemed to stir even though I couldn't feel any wind. He scanned the alley carefully.

"Come out," he said to us in heavily accented but clear English. "You have nothing to fear."

We stepped forward into the light. As I got closer, I could tell from how he stood, and a psychic shimmer in the air that his power went far beyond the muscles of his body.

"I know you," he said. "*Jin*, but not really *Jin*. He died, in Showa 18." He shifted his glare to Alex, and I did not like how his eyes fell on her curves. "And you're *shoji*." He turned his eyes to me, then turned his left hand upward to reveal his forearm. "You know me too."

In black ink just below his elbow was a mark like a tattoo, two symbols side by side just like those on my upper back. It was the mark of loyalty, of *Chuugi*. My mark. My eyes tracked up his building arm back to his face, and he smiled a fierce and terrible smile. "I am *Chuugi*. I am who you will become when you fully grow."

CHAPTER 13

Something strange ran through me, then, like when you hold a microphone too close to a speaker, only instead of with sound it was with...well, um...it was with whatever part of me made me...*me*. Every hair on my body stood on end for just a second. The warrior in front of me felt it too, I could see it in his eyes, but he just laughed.

After it passed, the other *Chuugi* said, "Well, come on then, *Jin*, me. Sensei's waiting." He turned and led us up the steps, into the dojo. Alex shrugged at me, and we both followed.

As we passed between the stone lion-dogs at the top of the steps, I saw chips and cracks in their faces and bodies. There were some of the same patterns I remembered from the statues at the door in Portland. A few I knew were missing, like the one on the left had both of its ears still, but these were the same statues. I wondered how Sensei had moved them across the Pacific Ocean, and when. I wondered what he would look like seventy years younger, closer to my age, maybe even younger than this other *Chuugi*.

Through the door, we came first into a small room with a table at the center, and every other available surface covered with jars, pots, bags of herbs, and bundles of dried plants. He led us through, into a larger room that made me gasp even though I was trying hard to be as cool and calm as the two older warriors with me.

The room was almost exactly the same as our dojo in Portland. It had the same dark beams and straw mats, the same low table in one corner. Punching bags and training dummies stood in a line along one wall. There were small differences, too. The weapons were mostly Japanese, instead of from all over the world like at home. The corner with our boxing ring had been replaced by a circular Sumo ring instead.

No. That wasn't right. In the future, a boxing ring would replace the sumo ring. Either way, the ring felt just as right in that space as what I was used to. The dojo *felt* the same. It was still my home.

One major difference caught my attention, filling my belly with a sick dread. Against one wall, seven stone lanterns stood on a heavy wooden shelf. Each was about the size of a basketball, and each was carved with the

Japanese characters for one of the seven virtues of Bushido: Duty, Courage, Honor, Compassion, Loyalty, Truth, and Courtesy. That part was the same as in my time.

The difference was, in my dojo, five of the lanterns were dark. The ones for *Makoto* and *Rei*, Truth and Courtesy, were still lit, glowing to guide the final lost Bushido Warriors to join us. Here, six of the lanterns glowed with a ghostly yellow flame. Only mine remained.

The other *Chuugi* shouted, "*Tadaima!*", which even I knew meant something like "Hi honey, I'm home!"

"*Chuugi?*" came Sensei's voice from the back room. It sounded exactly like it did in my time. "*Annatana no?*"

"*Hayaku kite!*" my future self's voice sounded urgent, but to us he smiled and winked. Alex whispered, "He told Sensei he's taken prisoners."

"*Fututabe?*" Sensei's voice sounded annoyed to me, even though I couldn't understand the words.

"*Hai, Sensei!*" the other *Chuugi* said. He winked at us again and gestured for us to sit at the low table. It felt the same, smelled the same, as the table at the dojo back home, even though I could tell from the grain and color of the wood that it was a different table.

Sensei's voice came again from behind the door to his room, "*Ikutsu?*"

"*Ni,*" said *Chuugi*, while holding up two fingers on his right hand for us to see.

A moment later, my mentor and teacher came through the door carrying a tray with two wooden boxes, some cups, and a steaming tea pot. As he knelt, he balanced the tray perfectly, sinking to his knees without rattling the cups or sloshing the water. He rinsed out each cup with water from the pot, pouring the fluid into one of the boxes as he finished each one. He breathed deeply, calmly, as he did so, concentrating his full self on the task in front of him. He opened the other box and used a tiny wooden spoon to measure matcha tea powder into each cup. He filled the first with a trickle of water, then the second.

Once he had served the three of us, he lifted his own cup and sipped with a long, loud slurp. He set it down, smiling with pleasure. Then he opened his eyes and looked at us.

I swallowed my tea. The warmth flowed into my belly, chasing out most of the fatigue and aches of the day. I set my own cup down and looked at Sensei. He nodded, then spoke.

"I received a visit like this one day ago, but you were forced to retreat," he told us in smooth but accented English. His face was like always, with a small smile like he was remembering a favorite joke.

"I tried to protect them, but they ran when the *oni* attacked," said *Chuugi*. He glowered and shook his fist like he was about to slam it on the table, but he stopped himself after Sensei shot him a look. He tucked his hand beneath the table, looking sheepish.

"But it didn't happen at all," I said. "We weren't here yest—"

Alex cut me off. "It probably did. We probably were."

"What? How?"

"We probably will?"

"We will?" I said.

"Verb tenses, *Chuugi*."

"*Nani*?" said the other *Chuugi*.

"No, the other *Chuugi*," said Alex. She and Sensei gave almost identical laughs at the confusion, not unkind but deeply enjoying the absurdity. I thought about it until I understood. Well, until I understood that Alex understood. I had rarely gotten in trouble trusting her to know what was going on.

"Where are you coming from?" Sensei asked.

"They came through the park," said *Chuugi*.

"Isn't the question when are we coming from?" I said.

Sensei replied, "I know you are from my future, or my past. Or maybe I am from yours?"

"How do you know?" I stammered. I always sort of assumed Sensei knew everything, but that was above and beyond.

"All of the warriors of this time, all but one, are dead."

"All?" Alex said. Her voice shook on even the single syllable.

"All but me," *Chuugi* said, beaming with solemn pride. I held out my fist for him to bump. He stared at it, confused, then inclined his head in a bow. I put my fist away, feeling stupid.

Sensei said to Alex, "All but *Chuugi*. From when do you come? I would suspect a trap. Our enemies move freely abroad, led by a force that has yet to reveal itself. But the war makes them all brave while it reduces our own numbers, and they do not need subterfuge. I am prepared to accept that you are both who you appear to be, but that you are not from this time."

Chuugi said something harsh-sounding in Japanese. Sensei spoke short, gentle sentences back to him. This continued for a while, with Alex looking concerned and me having no idea what was going on. At last, *Chuugi* bowed and opened his hands in invitation.

"*Chuugi* is less prepared to do so," Sensei said. He smiled gently, "he worries about the safety of an often foolish old man. But he has agreed to trust me in this."

Alex spoke then, in a language I didn't recognize. Sensei spoke back in the same language. I listened, but understood nothing more than a sense of deep sadness passing between them. The two old warriors were talking about shared sorrows, and heavy responsibility.

Across the table from me, *Chuugi* screwed up his face in concentration, looking back and forth between them. I said, "Can you understand them?"

"No," he said. "They are...the same?"

That's when it hit me. Alex, the future Alex, wasn't just Alex. She was Sensei Alex. At some time in in our lives, she would take on that responsibility, and replace the man sitting across from her. But that meant...I didn't want to think about that.

The tone in their voice, the vibration of sorrow, of having seen too much and done too little, made me want to cry at the same time it made me want to protect them both from every kind of hurt, from the death of a friend or skinning a knee or anything in between. I felt about them the way I felt about Mom whenever she looked sad at how hard our lives sometimes had to be.

Alex changed back to English. "About seventy years in the future for *Chuugi*. For this *Chuugi*. For me, nearly one hundred and sixty years."

Sensei nodded gravely. "A long journey. Do you need something to eat?"

"Thank you," Alex said. "*Arigato gozaimasu*, but no."

Chuugi and I shared a look that told us both the other didn't agree with the not eating part, but that we would let Alex and Sensei…well, um, Alex-Sensei and Sensei-Sensei continue.

Sensei said, "What brings you to me? You are welcome, of course."

At that moment, the lantern for Alex's symbol of *Jin* lit all by itself. Its warm glow joined the light from my lantern and pushed the shadows in that corner just a little further back.

"We are here for you, Sensei," Alex said.

"And what do you need from me?"

"We need you to go, Sensei. You must leave the city, and take *Chuugi* with you, as soon as possible."

"I plan to go. I was going to take the train yesterday."

"History says you already left," Alex told him. "Agents of an enemy from the future stopped you."

Chuugi spoke then, in rapid Japanese, his voice angry. Sensei nodded when he was done, and said to us, "We know. *Chuugi* himself spotted the spies on the train, and we returned here without boarding."

"Everywhere," *Chuugi* said. "Enemies in Asia. On great steel ships. Filling the skies with planes. Poisoning the Emperor's ear in Tokyo. Huddled in huts here in our city. Everywhere."

Alex said, "We understand you will be stopped again."

"Then I will leave another day. They cannot stop me forever, and the people of Hiroshima need me."

"Sensei," Alex said. "Something terrible will happen here in the morning. The Americans will attack Nagasaki, killing fifty thousand people."

"But what could kill so many?" Sensei's smile faded then, replaced by a look of shock and horror. His eyes darted to *Chuugi,* who nodded. They whispered together, "Hiroshima."

"Yes, Sensei," Fiel said gently.

He sighed, deeply, his eyes bright with unshed tears. "War is not like war when…"

"When, Sensei?" I said. *Chuugi* bristled in his space across from me.

"Not so long ago," Sensei said. The tears began to roll down his face. "Why? Why would they do that to us again?"

"Well…" I began. We had covered that in my history class the year before. Most people thought it was because the Japanese wouldn't surrender unless we proved we could do it more than once. A lot of other people think it was to show the Russians we could drop nukes as often as we needed to. I was ready to talk about it, but Alex pinched my leg and shook her head. I closed my mouth.

"*Shikata ga nai,*" she said.

Sensei smiled again, but his eyes still leaked tears. "I imagine I teach you that in a year yet to come?"

"*Hai,* Sensei."

"*Arigato,* Sensei."

We were all quiet then, alone together with our own thoughts. Only the buzzing insects from outside broke the silence.

"All right, Sensei," Alex said at last. She rose to her feet. "What things must you take with you? You already planned to go. Are your things packed? Our *Chuugi* isn't the sharpest katana on the rack, but he can carry a lot even for somebody as big as him, and it looks like your *Chuugi* might even be stronger. When does the next train leave?"

"*I-ie*," Sensei said. Japanese for "no."

"That's okay, Sensei," I said. I stood up, too. Blood rushed into my unfolding legs, giving me pins and needles I did my best to ignore. "I can help you pack." After all the moves my dad made me and Mom do, sometimes in a hurry, I was good at packing, and Alex was right. I could carry a lot. I gestured to the other *Chuugi*, "Come on, me, let's get to it."

He sat as still as Sensei, who said again, "*I-ie*."

"No, really, Sensei," I said. I'm happy to help. I want to help. Let me help."

"*I-ie*."

"What is it?" Alex said.

Chuugi stood up then, while Sensei sat, kneeling beneath the low table. He said, "No. He will not go. We will not go."

CHAPTER 14

"Wait, what?" I said.

"Sensei…" Alex began, but *Chuugi* raised one hand to stop her. She shook her head in an annoyed expression I had seen dozens of times from my Alex, but stopped talking.

Into the silence, Sensei said, "I cannot go."

"But," Alex stammered. "You…you need to. You have to."

Chuugi growled, "Sensei does not have to do anything Sensei does not wish to do."

Sensei was quiet. It felt like the whole world became quiet with him for a long breath of a moment, and then he spoke. "Alex, what is your name?"

"*Jin*, Sensei."

"And you, Connor Morgan?"

"*Chuugi*, Sensei." I tried to smile at this times's *Chuugi*, but he just glowered.

"The Bushido code has seven words," Sensei said. As he recited them, I felt gooseflesh rise on my arms and neck. Even though each word he spoke was Japanese, they were the same as when I heard them in English. They had power beyond the sounds they made in my mouth and ears. When he said *Chuugi,* my eyes locked with the other warrior of Loyalty, and we nodded to each other. Sensei finished by saying, "Those are the 7 values of the warrior, *hai*?"

"*Hai*, Sensei," Alex, *Chuugi*, and I said together.

Sensei said, "Where on that list is ego?"

"Uh..." I began. Alex stood silently beside me.

"Self-preservation?"

Neither of us said a word.

"Self importance?"

"Uh..." I said again. I saw where he was going with this, but couldn't see far enough to find a good argument against it.

Chuugi spoke, in a tone that said he was reciting something memorized, "A warrior lives always in the thought of death, prepared at all times to risk his life in the aid of others. Live like you have already died, and leave no regrets on the field of battle."

Sensei nodded. "I had planned to go to Hiroshima to ease the pain there, but why go so far when so much suffering will come to this place?"

"But you will die, Sensei," Alex said.

I had a horrible thought. "If you die, who will teach us?"

"Another Sensei always comes," he replied. He gazed serenely at Alex.

"But," Alex began. Suddenly a chirping came from her pocket. She pulled out her phone-but-not-a-phone device and her eyes widened. Outside, the wind began to blow with force. It reached through the windows and pulled at my clothes and hair like grasping fingers.

Sensei stood up so quickly I didn't see him rise. "You must go now."

"But..." I said.

Chuugi crossed to the exit doorway, beckoning to us. "You must go. Now."

"Yeah," Alex said, glancing at her gizmo again. "We kind of must."

"But Sensei," I said. Outside, the sudden wind battered our small shelter.

"Go," Sensei told us.

"Come," *Chuugi* said. We followed him out

We stopped at the edge of the park. *Chuugi* bowed to us each. "Good luck in your home."

Alex said, "We can't just leave him. He'll die!"

Chuugi shook his head. "It is not for you to decide when Sensei meets his fate! Arrogance is not part of the Bushido Code either!" He turned on his heel and stormed back toward the dojo.

The wind blew even harder as Alex led me to the park, but fell off completely when we passed the first line of trees. I wanted to ask about it, but could see from the look on her face that my friend was deep in thought.

When we stepped out of the park, the wind nearly slammed Alex into a nearby house. I caught her with one hand, and pulled her thin frame into my wind shadow. We kept moving. She checked her not-a-phone and guided us through the dark streets, following a different route than we had come from.

With each step away from the dojo, I felt my worry for Sensei grow. He was tough, and smart, and had survived much, but how could he be tougher than an atomic explosion? Alex stopped just after we crossed a brick bridge with two arches beneath it, then ducked through the shattered doors of a bomb-wrecked building. It was long and low, maybe a warehouse before it was destroyed. Inside was empty and dark, and then a ball of purple light appeared a few feet in front of us.

"So that's it, then?" I said to Alex.

"No! We have three more ripples. Three more tries!"

"Three more tries to do what?"

"Three more tries to change his mind!"

The gate expanded to its full size. At the center, through the tiny lens, I saw what looked like a row of lockers. It beckoned, the lockers zooming toward us until they were regular size and only a step away. Alex moved forward. I clenched my jaw, anticipating the pain about to hit us. The wind, which I thought we had left behind, picked up and blew ash all around.

"One!" Alex said.

"Two!" I shouted. I tried to say it with her, but the wind was so loud I couldn't hear for sure.

When she probably said *three*, we ran forward together and jumped into the gate.

CHAPTER 15

Coming through hurt just as much as before, but at the same time wasn't as bad. Like most kinds of physical and emotional pain, once you've survived it and learned to expect it, it just doesn't matter as much. I landed in the locker room, trying to roll out the impact but instead sliding on my face across the carpeted floor.

"Ow! Bad fucking word!" Alex shouted from somewhere behind me. I wriggled until I could see her. Through my still-blurry vision, I saw her on her knees below a wall clock. It was five minutes after noon. We had left a little bit after one.

"Hey," I groaned. I rolled onto my back, then did a kip-up into a standing position. I felt like somebody had loosened all of my joints with a wrench, then put them back just a little out of place. "It's an hour before we left the first time. Is that normal?"

Alex coughed for a while, then said, "Sometimes. Maybe? Time travel doesn't happen often enough for us to know what normal looks like. But I guess arriving earlier than you left isn't any weirder than, you know, travelling backwards through time."

I shook myself, breathed deep, and exhaled the last of the pain out of my body. Alex moved through a simple form to bring herself back to normal. She moved with a fluid grace I'd never seen before. I don't just mean I'd never seen it before from her. Alex was the most graceful person I had ever met. *My* Alex, from my time. The person in front of me moved like the most graceful person in the world had spent another half-century getting even more graceful. It was hypnotic, beautiful, and scary all at the same time.

When she stopped moving, she caught me gaping at her and blushed just a little. She hid her face behind her hair in a move just like the Alex I knew, and said. "If you think I'm something, *Chuugi*, you should see future you. A few years ago you threw a dump truck at a *tarrasque*."

"At a what?"

"A *tarrasque*. A dragon from French folklore. The look on its face..."

"What about Sage? Fiel? Galhardo?"

Alex smiled at me, sadly it seemed. "I can't tell you any more, old friend."

"Can't you tell me something? How many *The Raid* movies did they end up making?"

She made that zip your lip gesture, then mimed trying to swallow the key through lips already zipped closed.

"But—" I began.

"Connor Morgan and Angus Brawn, to mat four!" came a voice over the intercom. Just my luck. I arrived in time to wrestle a match after running and fighting for hours in another country and another time. The night's efforts settled over me like a heavy blanket, along with the two matches I'd already wrestled. Even though it was somehow earlier than when I'd left, five hours had passed in my personal time. I suddenly felt as tired as I ever had.

Alex winced in sympathy and hugged her face to my chest. "Go get him, tiger. I can't risk being seen."

"For you, Alex, I'll get him and bring selected bits back for you in a lunchbox."

"Ewww. Gross!" but she smiled, and said, "That's our Connor."

No matter how tough I was talking, I could barely move my legs when I turned and headed for the locker room door. But I walked, and kept walking, because that's what warriors do. They put one foot in front of the other when it's hard, when others won't, when the rest of the world turns back and runs the other way.

Soldiers, police, protestors, and all other warriors, that's what they do. Moms, too, and EMTs, and a lot of reporters and social workers. Sometimes I think that's what really makes somebody a hero. It's not the fighting, or the killing, or even the risk they take to protect the helpless. It's seeing the awful things cops see. It's living under the hardships that soldiers do. It's standing in front of riot police and saying what your conscience says you must. It's telling parents what EMTs and nurses sometimes have to in an emergency room. It's doing the hardest tasks and seeing the worst things in the world, so other people don't have to.

Warriors sometimes kill, and sometimes they have to die. But mostly warriors live in a world that needs warriors. And they live inside the truth of that world, so people can believe there's good there, too.

A collision bumped me out of those thoughts. Somebody said, "Sorry!" and squeezed past me through the crowd so quickly I almost didn't realize it was me. Well, not me. Me now, the normal time me. But I was here now, in normal time.

Wasn't I?

It was weird. Really, really weird. I watched myself jog toward the mat, and every part of me felt like he was some kind of imposter. Somebody in disguise. I wanted to run up and unmask him, like in the old cartoons with the dog and his stoner friend in the van. I almost chased him, but felt a strong hand take my shoulder. I turned, arcing my elbow to strike whoever had grabbed me.

Alex dodged the strike like I was moving in slow motion. "Hey," she said. "Easy there." She tried to pull me back toward the locker rooms, but I had a match to wrestle. I pulled in the opposite direction, dragging her a few feet until she shifted her weight and held me in place like an anchor.

"Dude," she said, "you have to come with me. Neither of us can be seen here right now. It's Friday."

"What do you mean, Friday?"

"It's Friday!"

"What?"

"I just saw a newspaper, and I confirmed it on my sonic screwdriver."

"Your what?" She pointed toward her not-a-phone thinger, which was hanging from her belt in a leather case. "Why do you call it that?"

She sighed. "That's not important now. Just never admit to Fiel that you asked that question. But it's Friday. We're not here an hour before we left. We're here twenty-three hours after."

"Friday?" I said. I glanced at myself walking out onto the mat. "I make it to Friday?" I smiled through all the exhaustion and weirdness. This was good news for me, for scholarships, for Mom.

"Apparently," she said. "Way to go, Connor. Come on. Let's go get some rest."

"No. Wait. I need to wrestle."

"Let the other you wrestle. That's why he's here, right?"

I worked that through my brain until I realized she was right. I nodded, but still turned back toward the mat. "I want to watch.

"Come on," Alex said. She pulled on my wrist some kind of joint lock that didn't hurt, but made me stumble away from the mat for a few steps before I recovered and stood my ground. One of the nice things about being as big as I am is I don't move when I don't want to be moved. Alex strained against me for a few moments more, then gave up and stood beside me.

I looked to the mat, over the heads of the people crowded around what they seemed to think would be a good match Coach was there, and Sage, and Mom was in the next line back. Mr. Waldron was there, too, standing just behind the main crowd and watching intently. He'd said he had contacts in UFC, so maybe he was thinking about recruiting me. Another reason to be happy I'd made it to Friday.

My stomach rolled with nerves as I watched myself shake hands with my opponent. I'd recognized the name when they announced the match, but it hadn't sunk in until I saw Angus standing across from the other me. He was 230 ropy pounds of stone badass who had beaten me the only other time we had wrestled. Angus was stronger than me, and more experienced, and wrestled for a team that liked to fight dirty.

Win or lose, this was going to hurt.

"Connor," Alex said. She was pulling on my arm again. "*Chuugi*, Connor. We should go."

"Why?" I said. It was weird watching myself wrestle. Coach sometimes recorded us so we could watch and find our mistakes, but that was different. Very different. So different I...um, well, I can't even think of a good way to describe how different it was.

Angus refused the shake. Mom put her hands to her mouth and shouted, "Make him eat that hand, Connor Morgan!"

"Like, right now, Connor," Alex said. "I think I just saw Susan making out with two guys and a *Penthouse* model. We should go check that out."

"What are you talking about, Alex?" I didn't turn to look at her. I was busy watching myself get headbutted off the whistle, and somehow rally to sprawl a double-leg and fight it. My own nose hurt from just seeing the cheap shot, but I couldn't tell if it was just sympathy pain, or something to do with how the guy I just saw get his schnoz crunched was me.

I got angry then, and angrier still, watching this guy wrench at my legs and abuse my hurt nose to try and take me down for the rest of the round. He failed because I hung tough, and I felt proud of me. At the mat's edge, Mom was covering her face, peeking through her fingers.

As the round broke, Angus skull-butted my jaw with the crown of his head. I would have fallen down if Sage hadn't come out to catch me. Coach immediately started shouting at the ref, and Angus's coach, and anybody close enough for him to notice. He was furious. Mom came up to me and checked my eyes with a flashlight.

She must have thought I was okay, because she let me go back out to wrestle my second round with Angus. He won the toss and started with us both up, then he punched me in the face as soon as the buzzer sounded.

"What the?" I shouted. I took a step forward, but Alex held me in place.

"Don't," she whispered into my ear. Her free hand pressed against the small of my back in a way that warmed my legs while at the same time making me not want to use them.

"What are you doing?" I demanded.

"I'll tell you later. We have to go. *Now*."

But I couldn't go. On the mat, the ref had tried to stop the match but Angus kept going. Without a second's pause, he stripped one hand from my face, pulled me into a fireman's carry, and stood up. He pressed my full body weight up and over his head.

"Brawn!" the ref shouted. I could barely hear him over the gasps and boos from the crowd all around me.

"Angus! What the hell are you doing?" Angus's coach ran onto the mat, but he was too late.

Coach Russell said the F-word. Lots of times.

Then Angus brought my entire body down to drop my spine onto his knee. The snap of my back echoed across the near-silent auditorium. *Oni* erupted from their shadows in the rafters, flying and swarming like bats.

It was a killing blow, meant to end my life. Everything moved in slow motion as Angus's coach and Coach Russell dogpiled the huge athlete, holding him to the mat while he struggled. Mom and another paramedic crouched over me, moving. I knew people were shouting, but I couldn't hear anything. The *oni* swarmed over the scene so thickly, I had to stop *looking* so I could see what was going on.

That was a mistake. Mom moved with a focused, furious energy I had only seen in her a few times, but I could feel the pain and fear radiating off of her even from my distance. I could only see my feet and half my shins, but they weren't moving. A year's worth of minutes passed, then Mom started to scream.

The sound filled my ears even as vomited filled my mouth, the fumes burning inside my nose and throat. I swallowed it down and tried to make sense of what I had just seen. Alex seemed tiny and far away as she took me by the arm and led me gently out of the auditorium.

CHAPTER 16

I stumbled through the crowd with the help of my friend, blind except for the image of Mom's anguished face. She kept her warm, comforting hand on my back as I emptied my stomach into a toilet.

It took a long time. Given how little I'd had to eat in the past few hours, you'd think I'd have run out of things to puke up. You'd think wrong. Every time I thought it was over, I'd see Mom's face again when Angus dropped my spine on his knee, and I'd find new things to get out of my belly.

Through the misery, Alex stood there softly saying my name over and over again. The strength and quiet, the peace in her voice worked through my ears and into my own mind. It was smaller than the cold rage and creeping horror that twisted in the rest of me, but it was stronger, too. It dulled the edge just enough for me to stop reacting, and start thinking.

At his worst, my dad would become an animal. He only reacted, never thought. That's how he would end up hitting my mom, and sometimes me. Thought wasn't a part of him in those moments. I'm not making excuses for him. I'm glad he's in jail, away from us, but it was a part of human nature I could understand. I knelt there, leaning my forehead against the cool porcelain, and let Alex's presence help me breathe my way back into a thinking mind.

"You knew," I said between wracking breaths that were equal parts sob and dry heave. "You knew that was going to happen."

Alex passed me a wad of toilet paper for my chin. "That's true. I knew. Kind of."

"What's *kind of* even mean, Alex?" Some of the anger in me surged in her direction, but I managed to keep it in check. I knew she wasn't responsible for what was happening around us, and even if she made mistakes, she made them for the best reasons possible. Still, I couldn't make myself look at her. I kept my eyes closed, my head hanging.

"It means I don't know much about how time travel works, but I know a little. When Sensei died in Nagasaki, and when you died today, things changed. It's not how it's supposed to be, either of those things. Most people don't remember how things were supposed to be when the flow of time changes, but some of us can. We can even access both sets of memories, feel them side by side. It's a lot like going insane, but the Abuelitas told me about these things."

"The Abuelitas?"

Alex laughed to herself. "I'm sorry, *Chuugi*. But I'll tell you when you're older. I promise."

"Can you tell me what they told you?"

"Yes, old friend. The right memories, the ones of how things were supposed to be, they feel more familiar. They feel more correct than the others."

I thought about that, about how wrong my death had felt. But then how wrong would it have felt if it was true? Then again, Alex had talked about me doing things much later. I wasn't supposed to die.

At last, I said, "So. You knew I died." My stomach revolted again at the memory of the snapping sound, and Mom's screams, but I held it down and breathed clean air until I was steady again. "You knew I died, but you also knew I didn't die."

"Yes," Alex said. Even though I couldn't see her face, I felt her sad smile in the pressure of her hand. "You're getting the hang of this."

"And you feel that way with Sensei, too?"

"Yes."

"But he dies in the future."

Alex's hand clenched tight on mine, but just for a moment. She said, slowly, "What makes you think that?"

"You're Sensei now, aren't you, Alex. Alex...um...Alex-Sensei?"

"Yes, Connor."

I turned now to face her, opening my eyes as I wiped my mouth clean. "He's not going to retire and go fishing in Bend. This is a lifetime job."

Alex slid out of the stall, leading me gently by my hand. As we moved to sit on nearby benches, she said. "Yes, *Chuugi*. Yes. He dies."

"And you knew his dying at that time was the right...well, um...the right...time? The right...way? The right dying?"

"Yes, that. That and..." she trailed off, shaking her head like a dog trying to get rid of a fly.

"That and what?"

She hid behind her hair for a moment, but I shifted my face so I could peek through the strands. After a moment, she parted her locks and faced me squarely. "There's a lot of stuff, and a lot of it's weird. I wouldn't want to accidentally drop some spoilers."

I laughed. It was a short laugh, with a wave of grief and anger crashing down on top of it, but it still felt good. I knew if I *looked* just then, its power would have driven away any *oni* creeping toward us. To Alex, I said, "Okay. But tell me this. When we fix things, I won't have died right now, right? And Sensei will still be alive to die when he's supposed to?"

"That's the idea."

"And I'll forget everything I just saw?"

"You'll forget most things, *Chuugi*. Sometimes you might feel a little deja vu, or have a really vivid nightmare. But yes. You will forget it because it never happened."

"And —" my voice cracked like it used to when I was eleven and getting my first real growth. "And for Mom.

For her, I won't ever have died? Right? She never, ever saw that if we can save the day?"

Alex's face softened. For a moment, I saw my younger friend just as clearly as if I'd been sitting with her. "Yes, Connor. She will never, ever see you die."

"But you won't forget?"

"No. I won't."

"Because you're a Sensei."

"Because of some parts of being Sensei. Other people can do it, too."

"Like the Abuelitas, whoever they are."

"I'm still not going to tell you, but yes. Like the Abuelitas."

We were quiet for a while, together, just sitting and breathing and taking comfort in one another's company. At last, I said, "Alex-Sensei?"

"Yes, *Chuugi*-Senpai?"

"This is all very confusing."

"Yes," she said. She put one arm around my shoulders, having to sit up and stretch a little to get all the way across.

I sighed. I was so tired, and confused, and sad, and afraid, and so much smaller than this person who could barely reach around my body.

"Alex-Sensei?"

"Yes, *Chuugi*-Senpai?"

"I'm really tired."

She pulled me toward her and reached up to hug me with her other arm. She cradled me as I didn't exactly cry, but just accepted the full weight of all that had happened since my last night of sleep. The exhaustion, the fear, the pain, the confusion. Those kids in Nagasaki.

Mom. Seeing myself die. I let it all course through my breaths, to work through me and over me. After a while, I'd breathed enough of it out so, mostly, only I was left. I whispered, "Thank you," to my friend as she continued to hold me.

"Shhh," she whispered back.

I did cry, then. I cried like when I was in kindergarten, when my feelings were so much bigger than the rest of me, when I didn't understand anything about the world except how much it hurt sometimes. I cried on the shoulder of a stranger who had been my friend for many times longer than I'd been alive, and after how long I did not know, I stopped.

"Thank you," I whispered. She didn't have to answer, and didn't even mention how wet I'd made her shirt with my tears, snot, and slobber.

The doors opened, and we pulled away from each other, looking toward the entry. Fiel and Galhardo strode in, their faces glowing with rage and glistening with tears of their own.

CHAPTER 17

I dove around the corner of the lockers, then slipped into the same bathroom stall I'd used to throw up. Alex-Sensei was right behind me, and we shut ourselves inside before the brothers could see us. She hadn't told me so, but I was pretty sure them seeing me a few minutes after they watched me die would be one of those bad time things she was so afraid of.

Normally, they would have spotted that kind of furtive movement. They're Bushido Warriors like me, and in the habit of noticing anything that might mean an ambush. But they were too filled with their own grief.

Fiel half-carried his brother, whose bad arm hooked awkwardly over his shoulder, to the bench I had shared with Alex a moment before. They collapsed there together, sobbing into each other in a pain I could physically feel. It made tears start up in my own eyes, seeing them hurting so much and thinking about how Mom, and Sage, and Susan must be in that moment. Even Sensei, not Alex-Sensei but my Sensei, would feel it. Without permission, my mind showed me a little movie of the sorrow on his face as my lantern re-lit on its shelf, and somehow painted that same heartbreak onto the face of my mother.

Oh, no. Mom. A new movie played, of Mom telling my dad I had died, and I suddenly felt the need to throw up again. I pushed the urge down and cried instead. Hot tears dripped off my face and onto the tile floor while my body shook with the struggle to keep quiet.

Alex's body shook beside and behind me. I don't know how long we were there, together but apart in our shared mourning, before I recovered enough to put my eye to the crack in the door and look out again at my friends.

The tear-blurred forms slowly shifted from sobbing, to quiet weeping, to talking in whispers. Then, in the space of an instant, something changed in them both. They grew cold, and pulled apart from each other. I didn't need to *look* to know some *oni* had gotten inside of them.

It had happened to me, too, with demons riding my frustration with my dad and some stupid jealousy about

Susan. They had almost pushed me to kill myself before Mrs. D. had driven them away.

"You know where he lives?" Galhardo said. Fiel pulled out his cell phone. It really did look a lot like the thing Alex-Sensei called a sonic screwdriver. He pressed and swiped on the screen.

"I do now," Fiel said.

"There's only one thing to do, then." They got up and walked out, their every movement smooth and without emotion. Predatory.

I dried my face on my arm, and cleared the snot out of my throat and nose. Alex-Sensei opened our stall door.

"They're going to go murder Angus, aren't they?" I said.

"That seems likely," Alex said to me.

"We should stop them," I said.

"Let me tell you a story Sensei tells us all over tea a year or so from now. I think it won't hurt anything. A long time ago, a Bushido warrior watched as all six of the others died in a war like the one we're fighting now. It could even be the same war. When the last of his friends died, an *oni* got inside of him and broke him completely."

"They killed him?" I asked.

"Worse. They turned him. He joined their side, and he was so angry he lived the rest of his life sure he was right."

"So we should stop them," I said. I'd felt what it was like to not be stopped, then to be stopped, with the oni inside me, for only about a day. I couldn't imagine a lifetime of that.

"Maybe we won't have to," Alex said.

"What? How?"

"This wasn't supposed to happen. If we save Sensei, we might stop your murder. If we stop your murder, Galhardo and Fiel won't ever want to kill Angus Brawn."

"Does it work like that? Can we do that?"

"We can try. The next gate is in…" she checked her sonic screwdriver and made a face. "Ten minutes. We have to hurry."

"And you're sure that's a better move than staying here to stop Fiel and Galhardo from ruining Angus's day? And, you know, themselves?"

"I'm not sure. Being a Sensei means rarely being sure about anything. But I am confident. This is our best chance at success."

"Okay," I said. I wiped my eyes, nodded, and said again, "Okay." When I stepped forward, though, Alex put a hand on my chest, stopping my motion before it really began.

"*Chuugi*," she said, "Connor, are you good to go?"

"Yeah. Sure. I'm good."

She slid into my vision and looked up at me with eyes so much older than my friend's. "No. Really. You just saw an incredibly hard thing to see. You might be the only person in the universe to ever have seen that. If you want to stop it from happening, you must be one hundred percent okay nine minutes and twenty-three seconds from the end of this sentence. Remember, the resistance will only get worse the further along we go."

"What?" I said. "Why?"

"They'll have had more time, in that time, to collect their resources."

"That's —" I closed my mouth, opened it, closed it, then opened it one last time to say, "I don't even know that I know what you just said."

Alex smiled. "That's all right, *Chuugi*. Just be ready for it to get harder from here. Things could be bumpy on the other side of the gate."

I thought about that, and breathed. I remembered what had just happened, and what might happen if we failed. "Whoever's on the other side of that gate just killed me, and made Mom cry. Let's get bumpy."

CHAPTER 18

The time between jumping into the gate and landing on the other side stretched. I had space to think about Mom, and Susan. About how they had looked when they saw me die. A pang of guilt ran through me at not being there to comfort them at that moment, for not telling them I'm not really dead. But what I was doing instead would mean they never needed that comfort.

At least that's what I thought would happen. I hoped I was right.

When I landed, I stayed on my feet despite the pain in my gut and joints, and the swirling dizziness behind my eyeballs. I wobbled and stabilized myself in a kung-fu stance Alex had taught me. Then something punched me in the neck and I fell down anyway.

I landed on my hands and knees, blind and confused for a moment. Bodies hit me on the waist, back, and shoulders, driving me to my stomach. *Oni*, dogpiling me. Not one of them was larger than a cat, but there were so many their weight was more than I could handle. Somewhere beyond them, Alex shouted in pain.

I rolled hard onto my back, crushing some oni and scattering the rest. A neck bridge into a sit-up got me halfway free. Two more *oni* leapt at me from nearby, but I clapped my hands to sweep them into each other. They popped like nasty balloons. I let out a raw scream of rage and triumph, roaring into the night. It felt so good, crushing the enemies who wanted to kill me, to make Mom cry. I struck out again and again, not with punches so much as ripping, clawing hands that tore the demons into ribbons as I half-laughed with the sheer joy of it. This was better than any wrestling match. These were real monsters, who wanted to do real damage, who I was really destroying.

A few feet away, Alex was on her knees with demons scrambling on her neck and shoulders. I shuffled to her and ripped off one that looked like a tortoise with bat wings, then a pair of snakes linked by spider's legs, then another, and another, until she was free and rolled to her feet.

"Thanks, *Chuugi*!" she shouted as we shifted into a V, our backs to each other but facing toward the mass of our enemies.

There were so many they seemed more like a single, huge shadow than a group of smaller demons. They pressed toward us and we gave ground until our heels found a cliff behind us. The rush of water sounded from somewhere below, carrying with it a rancid stink and sharp chemical tang.

The first wave of demons crashed into us. We stood our ground, ripping them into ribbons of shadow and raw, reeking smoke, or tossing them off the cliff and into the water below. The splashes came less than a second after each fell, telling me the water wasn't far below.

Alex panted as she flung another demon into the air. "You thinking what I'm thinking?"

I eyed the remaining demons. There were dozens left, *oni*, and *tanuki*, and other forms I didn't have a name for yet, all regrouping for another charge. "Why is it I always end up jumping off high places when I'm with you guys?"

"One time! One time that happened! And I wasn't even there!" Alex's leg shot out with an almost invisibly fast kick, spearing a charging *oni* and bursting it. The demons behind skittered away, but only just a little.

"Really?"

"Well, up to now. I think. It's been a while but I'm pretty sure that's right. Have you been to the Grand Canyon yet?" As the next wave came in, she dropped to her hands with a leg sweep that passed through three like they were made of cotton candy. She rode the momentum into a one-handed somersault dive off the cliff.

"Show off!" I shouted, as I grabbed the nearest *oni* with both hands and stepped backward off the cliff. As I fell, I turned so it was beneath me when I hit the water. It squeaked in terror, then popped into smoke that smelled almost as bad as the river. I was able to take one last, gasping breath before the stinking flow closed over my head.

I tumbled in the stream, spinning in the current, blind and struggling to keep my mouth above water. My head slammed into something hard. A rock, maybe, or a piece of wood. I couldn't tell. My vision blurred, but I forced it to straighten. Or at least to straighten as much as it could while bouncing in murky water and yellow foam.

Alex's voice came over the rush, from someplace nearby. "Put your feet downstream! Hit rocks with your legs, not your head!"

I twisted in the rolling current until I managed that. Once I had my back to the flow, its pressure pushed my head and chest upward enough I could see her graying head bob just a few yards ahead of me.

We rode the waves, fending off rocks and debris with our feet and scanning the shoreline for places to climb out. But there was only rocky, muddy cliffs on either side. The current swept us through the bridge we had crossed on our escape the last time, and almost slammed me into the center post. At the last moment, I kicked off of the bricks and sent myself spinning beneath the span.

That must have given Alex an idea, because at the next bridge she grabbed one of the supporting poles. She caught me as I passed, but my weight pulled her into the water with me. I flailed with my free hand and caught the last pole on the opposite side, then reeled Alex in an inch at a time. We pulled ourselves, squelching and stinking, up the support timbers until we lay on the bridge itself, gasping for breath in the fouled air.

"They're responding," Alex said after a while. "They know what we're doing."

I inhaled to talk, and the stink made me cough. When I had it under control, I said, "Can we bring more people next time? Can we bring all of us?"

"Maybe one," Alex gasped. "After." She stopped short and retched over the side of the bridge. "If we make it home."

"Shhh," I said. I jerked my head toward the street on one end of the bridge. Four shadows were marching past. The tallest seemed unsymmetrical, and the shortest carried a lantern on a pole. They walked slowly past the bridge, and further into the city. We stayed silent, in the shadows, until they were out of sight.

Then, legs weak and dripping with foulness, we moved into the night. We crept through the neighborhoods, past buildings burned and shattered by earlier bombing raids. My heart hurt for whoever had lived in those houses. They were families. Moms who loved their sons like Mom loves me. They had possessions, memories, and a feeling of safety in those houses, all now ruined by the blast.

Most of them had probably lived in those houses their whole lives. Maybe their families had lived there for generations. I knew how I felt about losing my apartment after just a few months. I couldn't imagine what that felt like. War is horror, even when it's just and necessary. It's pain, and suffering, and fear, even for the winning side.

As we reached the park, I said to Alex, "Is this what the enemy is planning for us?"

She gave me a questioning look, and I waved my hand around to indicate the ruined city we had just passed through. Her eyes widened in understanding, then narrowed. "I can't tell you that. It could change time."

"I call bull," I said. "We're here to change time. You came back because you wanted to change time."

"No, *Chuugi*. I'm coming back to stop the bad guys from changing time. I'm *restoring* time. If I could change time, don't you think I'd go back to earlier and stop a war that killed millions?

"A war like that's coming?" I gasped. I imagined Portland in ruins, my Mom starving, the dojo broken like the homes behind us. "Is...is that how Sensei dies?"

"No," Alex said in the tone her younger self used when scolding me for trying to pun with Galhardo and Fiel. "This one. The one we're in right now. World War Two. I would stop World War Two."

"Oh," I said, feeling dumb. I shut up and walked through the park. A few steps later, something else occurred to me. "Hey, Alex? Um...Alex-Sensei?"

"Yes, *Chuugi*?" her voice still carried amusement from my earlier mistake. She almost sang her response.

"What time is it?"

"It's a little after midnight here, why?"

"So, we must be right ahead of us, then?" I had no idea what time it was the first time, when we had met the other *Chuugi* and spoken to Sensei, but the sky was lighter and it felt earlier in the day.

"Yes," Alex said. I peered through the darkness across the cobblestone street in front of the dojo. It looked so much like the one at home, with its simple staircase and two stone dogs guarding a small, unadorned door.

"My head hurts," I whispered.

"Time travel will do that."

As we crouched in the alley, a large figure stalked out of the park and crossed the little square in a line toward the dojo. I recognized from his walk, and the zing of feedback running through me, that it was the other *Chuugi*, on his way to speak with Sensei. When he was halfway there, Alex stepped out of our hiding place and shouted, *"Chuugi!"*

"Chuugi! It's us! *Jin* and *Chuugi!"*

His face shifted in an instant from careful confusion to absolute rage. His jaw set like iron. Anger flashed in his eyes. He bounded toward us, landing softly within kicking distance of us both. He was smaller than me, both shorter and with less muscle, but I could tell from how he moved that he was much more powerful. He took a fighting stance, his hands in fists and his legs bent, ready to spring.

"Jin is dead, imposter! And only I am *Chuugi!"*

CHAPTER 19

"Wait! Wait! *Matte! Matte!*" Alex shouted. She held her hands up and crouched into a posture that made her look even smaller than she usually was. *Chuugi* stood ready, but didn't attack. Not yet, anyway. I stepped out of the shadows to show myself. His eyes widened as he took in my height and size. I'm very big for 21st century high school. In 1940s Japan, I must have looked like a giant.

"This is not a trick," Alex said, her voice a calm whisper.

"That is what a trickster would say," *Chuugi* growled. His eyes darted between us as he shifted his stance to be ready to attack in either of our directions.

"No. We come from a different time. We are here to help. *Look* at us, and see what is true."

The warrior paused and gazed at us both, carefully and with more than his eyes. After a moment, he nodded once. "Why have you come?" I breathed a sigh of relief, but at the same time something nagged at me. Something I wasn't seeing.

"We have come back because we must speak with Sensei," Alex said. She wasn't shouting, but something in her voice made it carry across the square.

"No. Sensei cannot be disturbed. He is too…diminished…by the deaths of my brothers." *Chuugi* half-turned away from us, every motion a dismissal. Something else moved, in the shadows, near the corner of my eye. Something sneaky and dark.

"I cannot allow that," Alex replied, shouting now. *Chuugi* turned to face her fully, coiling his weight to spring just as I recognized the movement in the shadows: *oni.* So many they weren't hiding in the shadows, but made up the shadows themselves. In the dim light of the moonlit square, Alex and the other *Chuugi* faced each other like gunslingers, completely tuned out from the danger creeping close.

"Oni!" I shouted, never at a loss for just the right thing to say. Before I finished the word, Alex spun to face me and *Chuugi* leapt in one bound to the top of the dojo stairs.

The *oni* advanced in a tightly packed line. I threw a rock at one of them. It hit the demon so hard, it, and the two behind it, that they all popped and vanished. Others immediately filled their spaces. The supply seemed endless, and my heart sank. Beside me, though, Alex was smiling. I kept an eye on the monsters while shooting her a questioning glance.

"What happens to us in just a little while?" Alex asked. The demons took another step toward us. Three more, and the fight would be on. They seemed to be ignoring the dojo, and the other *Chuugi* standing guard at the door, entirely.

"Uh, we get our butts kicked by a million demons?" I said. Three of them broke from the line in a tight wedge. I sprang forward and smacked the two on the outside with wide sweeps of my arms, slamming them together on the one in the middle. They all vanished in puffs of reeking, eye-watering smoke. *Chuugi* did not move, just stood there on the stairs watching the battle, leaving all the *oni* free to focus on us.

"No. What happens to us a few hours ago, right here, and just a little bit after now?"

I shuffled backward, giving ground, as an eight-tusked elephant the size of a housecat trumpeted hate and pain at us. Alex's question confused me, but then I got it. "Riiight. We talk to Sensei right here, in just a little while."

"I knew you'd get there," Alex said. She threw out another swift, brutal kick and decapitated a demon that had stepped a little ahead of the pack. "And what will Sensei tell us then?"

"About how we ran away before he could talk to us."

"Exactly," Alex said. The octotuskephant charged at us with a sort of psychic howl. Alex dropped and swept its legs, then kneed it in the back of the skull. It exploded. Still, *Chuugi* did nothing.

I eyed the massive wall of demons poised to charge. If we stayed put, they wouldn't hesitate for long. "Uh, we should do that then?"

Alex said, "Yes. Let's." She leapt backward into the park and I followed. Behind us, I could feel the power of the demons surging up like surf gathering for a wave, but we made it through before the crash came.

We sprinted through the park so quickly I was afraid we might not notice ourselves coming the other way, but I never caught sight of us. I panted to Alex, "Now what?"

"We go to the next gate. Get back to your time. Figure it out."

On the other side of the park, we slowed to a gentle trot. We moved silently through the streets, passing the wreckage of this earlier war. A little before the bridge I'd come to know and sort of like, we heard the footsteps of a guard patrol and dove into the sooty remains of a bombed-out house. A moment later, a patrol of five guards in loose uniforms walked into view. It wasn't One-arm and his crew, but they carried with them the same proud, hungry, despair. They stopped to lean against a mostly intact shop front, gathering in their lantern light and whispering as they passed a small skin of a drink between them.

I watched them for a while, then whispered to Alex, "What do we do now?"

Alex whispered back, "we wait." She sat down cross-legged on the blackened floor, making no more noise than a butterfly.

"Do we have time?"

"We're not in that much of a hurry. We can make it if this is just a rest for them." I made more noise than a butterfly as I sat, but not so much the guards heard me.

We sat like that while the guards finished their rest. Above us, through the ruined roof, I could see the stars. They looked just the same. And Earth probably didn't look much different to them now than it did during my time, or the time when Alex was a sensei.

When the guards had walked on, and the last echoes of their footsteps had faded, I whispered again, "Hey, Alex?"

"Yes, *Chuugi?*"

"Do Susan and I end up married?"

I couldn't really see her face in the darkness, but I could feel the look she gave me just fine. She didn't say a word as she stood up and wiped the grime of the burnt building from her pants.

"Hey, Alex?"

"Yes, *Chuugi?*"

"What are we going to do?"

Alex breathed deeply, in the way Sensei had taught us both. I could almost see the exhaustion flow out of her as she did. My friend was very, very tired. "Well, there are two more ripples in the time stream. We can try two more times."

"What will we do differently on the next two, Alex-Sensei?" What we'd done so far hadn't worked.

"I don't know. I need to think. We need more information. Something's wrong, and I can't see what it is. We need more time."

"When do the other ripples bring us here?"

"Later tonight, and very early tomorrow morning. Like, still in the dark early."

She sighed to herself. I stopped asking questions. In that moment, so far from everything we knew, Alex didn't need her student. She needed her friend. I put my hand on her shoulder and held it until she turned her eyes toward me.

"You will figure it out. We will figure it out."

"Maybe," she said. She smiled despite the despair and exhaustion just behind her eyes. "We just need more time."

"What if we made some?"

"That isn't how it..." she paused then, her whole face wrinkling with thought. "Wait."

"What?"

"I have a crazy idea." She pulled out her sonic screwdriver and started tapping on it like a middle schooler playing *Flappy Birds*.

"You? Isn't that usually Fiel and Galhardo's thing?"

"Also Sage," she said, not looking up from her tapping. Don't you remember when she set fire to that pteranodon?"

"Uh, no."

"Damn. I did it again, didn't I?"

"Why did Sage set fire to a dinosaur?

She didn't answer, just led me out of the ruined house, through a narrow alley wet with rainwater, and down a mostly dirt road until we were outside of town, lying against a low ridge under a thicket of broad-leafed trees. The buzzing insects sang in the dark as she checked her sonic screwdriver once more, put it in her pocket, and said, "Now, we wait."

"Wait for what? What's going on?"

"We're taking a shortcut."

"Oookay," I said. "A shortcut to what?" In front of us, a gate appeared, its purple light throbbing above a small clearing. Alex stood up and started to run.

"Wait, Alex! A shortcut to what?"

She giggled in a very un-Sensei-like way as she led me through.

CHAPTER 20

I landed hard on sand in the middle of the loudest sounds I had ever heard. The roaring resolved into gunfire and screams as I rolled out the pain from the jump and suddenly felt colder than I had in a long time. I tried to stand up, but somebody swept my legs and I fell on my back next to Alex. Above us, white and bright yellow lines kept zipping over us. It took me a few breaths to realize they were tracer rounds, and lots of them. They buzzed like deadly insects, filling the air.

Without rising, I turned my head to the left and the right. We were on a beach, crawling with wet soldiers in green uniforms and round helmets all struggling to reach the dry sand while machine guns swept them from somewhere inland out of my vision. I had never seen so many people in one place, or so many bodies. The dead were everywhere, piled so high in some places other soldiers were taking shelter behind them. I looked back to Alex, hoping she would make sense of it all.

"Wait for it," I think Alex said. Her mouth made those shapes, but there was so much screaming and gunfire I wasn't sure. She lay there, so still and with such intensity I knew it was on purpose. Her mouth moved again: "Three, two, one..."

Something huge exploded very close to us. Sand and screams filled the air, but Alex was up before the sand had stopped falling. She sprinted toward the explosion and jumped into the hole it had left in the earth. My body didn't want to follow her, wanted to lie very still so maybe the bullets and the bombs wouldn't notice me, but I could not abandon my friend.

I screamed, roaring like I had when I fought the demons on the cliff, and the act of screaming helped my body make that first move. Soon, I was crouched, half-running, half-crawling past dead and living soldiers until I reached the hole.

Alex wasn't inside, but a pulsing, purple gate lay at the bottom. I knew where she'd gone, and what she wanted me to do.

"Shortcut?!" I shouted before I remembered she wasn't there to hear me. I would half to tell her on the other side. I rolled over the edge and fell way further than the bottom of the pit. The feel of the jump turned my brain and body inside out, then back again, before I landed hard on a flat, solid surface that felt like a floor. I closed my eyes against the fading pain, but could feel Alex there next to me.

"Ow! Alex! What was that?" My voice echoed in a place that felt utterly silent compared to the thunderous chaos of where we had been.

"A shortcut."

I wanted to answer, but it was so quiet it felt like saying anything else would be wrong. I opened my eyes and looked around, finding myself in a wide, glass-walled corridor. It stretched in both directions farther than I could see, with no people, no sound, no movement anywhere. On the other side of the walls was a city of domes, connected by hallways I guessed were a lot like the one we were standing in. Nothing moved out there, either. We were completely alone.

Alex looked at me, checking I was ready to go. I nodded, and trotted behind her as she led the way down the hallway. We followed it for at least a mile before she turned off into another dome, and we saw nobody the entire way. The sounds we made, each step and movement, somehow amplified the silence as they echoed through the lifeless place.

"Alex," I whispered. I spoke as quietly as I had when we were hiding from the guards, but it was so loud here it echoed. My voice distorted and came back: the ghost of my voice in the dead body of a city. "Is this real?"

Alex whispered back, "You're walking through it. You tell me."

"But is it real, real? This is the future?"

"Yes about the future, and no about the real real. It's not supposed to be this way."

My stomach clenched from the horror of what she was implying. "What happened? Can we stop it? How long do we have?"

"A genetics experiment, I don't know, and 284 years."

Another silent, still mile later, she led me through broad doors into an amphitheater at least a quarter-mile across. At the center of the bottom stood another gate, swirling and pulsing in this empty, lifeless space. As we picked our way down the tiers, I said, "Does it hurt more and more with every jump? Cos that last one hurt way more."

"This is the first time I've tried this, too. So, probably?"

"You're not going to lie to me this time?"

She didn't answer. I braced myself as we walked side by side into the twisting, purple maw.

What felt like hours of pain later, I slammed into a wall and felt the drywall break from my impact. I rolled to look, finding a shopfront. Its windows were busted out, and most of the shelves trashed, but it had probably been a coffee place once. Outside, through the empty window pain, an angry crowd roiled, chanting under floodlights.

Alex was right beside me, she shout-whispered into my ear, "We have to be fast. This is a tight connection. The gate is across the street."

"That street?" I shouted back. "The one with the angry mob and the angrier cops?" A bottle broke against the wall outside. I couldn't tell who had thrown it.

"Yes. You're going to have to go full Fezzik."

"Who's Fezzik?"

"You're Fezzik."

"But why?"

"Ask Fiel."

"Okay. But what does that mean?" Outside the crowd started a chant with a new rhythm. I couldn't understand the words.

"It means you're going to clear the way for me, and I'm going to run behind you."

"Through the mob?"

"Yes. Through the mob."

"It's not going to be easy."

"What ever is?"

It was actually pretty easy. We jumped through the open window and I moved at a half-run, half walk across the street. Most of the crowd was focused on whatever was in front of them, so they weren't ready for my 220 pounds hitting them from the side. By the time anybody was ready to deal with me, I had already busted through with Alex there in my wake. We reached the other side, and Alex pulled me into a doorway with a flat, black, steel door. She picked the lock, then we were inside a pitch black stairwell. I started to climb, but Alex held my arm. "No. It's right here. You were just faster than I expected."

I leaned against the door, feeling more than hearing the thrum of the crowd outside. It felt like the ocean.

"Hey, Alex?" I said, after a few seconds.

"Yes, *Chuugi*?"

"If we win, I won't remember any of this, right?"

"Right. What does that have to do with right now?" The stairwell suddenly lit up with a purple glow as the gate appeared, right where Alex said it would.

"Then I won't remember to ask Fiel why I'm Fezzik."

"I'll see what I can do about that. Some knowledge is important." The gate formed completely and we stepped through.

A while later, my body still wracked from the cramps of the jump, I said, "Hey, Alex?"

"Yes, Connor?"

"Is that—"

"No. Absolutely not."

"But I'm sure that's..."

"Stop looking. Come on. Last one."

"Promise?"

"No, but I think so."

"And you're sure that isn't — "

"Shhhh."

"Will it hurt?"

"What do you think?"

By then, I didn't think it would hurt. I knew it would, but I jumped anyway.

CHAPTER 21

We came through the gate into an alley I didn't recognize.

After the ashes of the house and sandy, bloody beach, not to mention our swim through the polluted river, we looked and smelled like a pair of young hobos. Well, I looked like a young hobo. Alex just looked like a hobo. We'd found my dad like that once, when I was in middle school. He came home covered with what looked and smelled like the goop that drains down to the bottom of trash cans in restaurants. He couldn't remember how he'd gotten so nasty, but Mom made him strip all the way to naked in our tiny backyard so she could hose him off. I never saw those clothes again, which made me sad at the time because his t-shirt was one of those *Big Johnson* joke shirts that made my eighth grade self laugh every time I saw it.

I tried to keep on my feet, but I collapsed onto the pavement. The street was almost as nasty as I was. Alex flopped down next to me, with a little more grace than I did.

"Last one?" I wheezed.

"Last one," Alex whispered, "for now."

We lay there for a while, just breathing and waiting for the pain to subside. I almost fell asleep, or passed out, or died, or something, but Alex kicked me gently back awake.

"Where are we?" I gasped. "When are we?"

"It's late on Tuesday night. We have just enough hours to grab some sleep, come up with a plan, and save the world."

"Could you say that again, slowly, like I was really dumb before I got confused by time travel and you had a bunch of gates beat me up?"

"It's late on Tuesday night. Our next gate leaves on Thursday morning, so we have about a day and a half. We needed time to figure things out. I found us some."

I stretched, the way you do after a long nap, and felt all my bones pop and creak. It hurt, but that good way stretching hurts instead of the way the gates hurt. That hurt like having extra versions of me, all wrapped up in the same skin and sharing our bones. My vision filled with stars as I stood up and said, "Okay. What do we do first?"

"Shower," Alex said. "We definitely need a shower."

She was right about that. You know you smell bad when you can smell yourself smelling bad. But where were we going to shower? I couldn't go home without some weird time stuff happening. Mom would see me. This Mom didn't think I was dead, but what if I was already home? Knowing me, the me at home right now would assume I was some kind of *oni* impostor and beat me down the second he saw me, like the *Chuugi* from the past almost did to me and Alex. Alex couldn't go home, either. Her family probably wouldn't even recognize her.

As if she read the questions in my mind, Alex said "Ponderosa. We'll go to school."

I'd never walked from the Moda Center to Ponderosa before, but I knew the route the way you do in a city you've been in for a bit. You know where you are, you know basically where your destination is, and you just work out the middle part as you go along. As we moved through the city, it all seemed so bright, so busy, compared to the silent, waiting darkness of Nagasaki. We passed people once in a while, and they moved with so little care. Portland was a happy city, at least by the standards I'd spent time in over the past couple days.

It was also impossibly bright. Streetlights, stoplights, neon signs, lights strung up in front yards, and headlights lit up the streets as we walked through them. Compared to the blackout conditions of Nagasaki during the war, it was almost dazzling.

When Ponderosa came into sight, I thought about another time I needed to get in after hours. I'd been alone, mostly naked, and freezing. I didn't know a good way inside back then, and I was highly motivated in that moment.

I nudged Alex, who had been walking in thoughtful silence beside me. "Alex?"

"Yes, Connor?"

"How are we going to get in?"

She didn't say anything, but led me over to the garage doors of the auto shop. She did...something...to the handle, then lifted it open. Ducking into the empty shop bay, she said, "I sabotaged the lock for emergencies two years ago."

"Ponderosa's still here then?"

She grinned, "No. Two years ago in this time."

"But that would mean—"

"That, *Chuugi*, would mean I am supremely prepared and not to be trifled with."

I thought about that as I ducked through the door and shuffled through the auto shop and into the school. It was exactly the kind of thing the Alex I knew would have done. "Fair enough."

Coming out of the auto shop and into the school halls, I felt safe. We were after hours, but people were at the school all the time for activities, and I was pretty sure I wasn't already on campus. If I remembered right, by that time on Tuesday night I was at the dojo. Later on, I'd come home to find Mom had tried waiting up, but fallen asleep on the couch with her face half-covered by a copy of an old Cherie Dimaline novel. I'd moved the book, tucked her in, and gone to bed.

So, that me was safe and sound and far from here as I waved goodbye to Alex, walked into the locker room, threw my clothes directly into the trash, and stepped into the shower. As the hot spray washed over me and muddy gunk swirled down the drain, I could see bruises from the last few days on my arms, legs, and trunk. They ran a rainbow of pain from yellow, to purple, to black, and I couldn't tell which came from my matches, which from fighting demons, and which from getting beaten up by a river in the mid 1940s.

When I was done with the soap, I stayed under the hot spray, letting it run over my muscles as I stretched some of the soreness out of them. It burned across the scrapes and cuts, but I could feel it helping with the fatigue and the strain. I would need some ice and some of Alex's salve, but I still felt better than I had since before I'd learned time travel was a thing.

Eventually, probably too late for Alex but too soon for my abused body, I turned off the water and grabbed a towel from the big plastic bin just outside the shower room. I wrapped it around my waist, then grabbed another to dry off with while I...Oh. Oh, no.

My clothes were in the trash can, so foul I could smell them from across the locker room. Normally I'd have a change in my locker, but they were all in my gym bag back at the Moda Center. No. That's where I'd left them half a day before. No. Where I'd left them a couple of days from now. Right now, they'd be home in my room, packed and ready for the tournament.

Which meant the damp towel was all the clothes I had.

I checked the lost and found. It was full of clothes, but nothing that fit me. I weigh in at 220 pounds, which is big for adults. I found a hoodie and a pair of jeans shorts, both of which were almost too small to squeeze into, and walked into the hall like...well, um...like some guy wearing mismatched clothes that were way, way too small for him.

Alex was waiting for me in the hall, leaning against the opposite wall like Susan would after practice sometimes. She didn't even laugh at me as she threw a bundle of clothes at me. "Hey there, Hulk smash. They're your size."

I caught them with one hand even while my mouth said, "Wait, what?"

"I keep something in everybody's size in my locker. You know, just in case."

"You what now?" I eyed the bundle. They were simple, navy blue sweats, plus a t-shirt, socks, and some underwear, and exactly in my size.

"Somebody has to. Besides, what did I just tell you about being supremely prepared and not to be trifled with?" She waved at me in a gesture that was one half "bye-bye" and the other half "shoo!".

Five minutes later, I was warm and comfortable in my new clothes and we were walking through the night. We took the same route I usually did going from wrestling practice to our dojo, through the city that still felt unbelievably bright and happy in ways it hadn't before. We settled into the alley across the street, where we had fought demons together the night I had first met Alex, and learned about the war against the demons.

The front of the dojo looked like it always had, and weirdly like it did in Nagasaki more than seventy years earlier. *Ah* and *Um*, the two dog guardian statues, stood at the top of the steps on either side of the solid, red door. I couldn't see the training floor from outside, unlike many of the dojos I'd seen around town, but I could hear the occasional *kiai*, and I could almost physically feel the energy radiating off the building. It was warm, and solid, the way few things are. It was my home.

"What now?" I asked .

"We wait." Alex checked her sonic screwdriver, then said. "It will be a while. Get comfortable."

We slipped further into the shadows and sat together in a comfortable silence. As we waited, my eyes and mind wandered to the eaves where demons had rained down me, Fiel, Galhardo, and Sage my first night as a Bushido Warrior, and to the roof where I had first learned how to *look*, and to the park behind us. There was a park next to the dojo in Japan, too.

I'd almost died in both of those parks. I'd almost died tonight. I was going to die in three days unless we figured out how to save Sensei and turn the time back to normal time. And even if I did fix all of that and survive, Mom and I still had an eviction to worry about. I'm big, and I'm pretty strong, and I can keep moving forward better than almost anybody I know, but eviction law wasn't something I could help Mom with.

Almost like she read my mind, Alex silently put one strong, slender hand on my shoulder. I smiled despite it all, and relaxed into her friendship. Time passed like that until the dojo door opened and I could see my friends framed in the light. Galhardo and Fiel came first, moving with a similar stride even with Galhardo's limp. I was right behind them, filling almost the entire doorway with my bulk. I don't usually see myself like that, next to people from the outside, and it still surprises me. In my mind, I'm mostly the little kid I'd been during the years I was growing up, even though I can see the tops of most peoples' heads now. Alex laughed silently to herself when her thin, younger frame glided through the light and down the stairs.

Sage was the last to leave, with Sensei shutting the door behind her. When her car lights turned the far corner and out of site, Alex led me silently out of the shadows and across the street. I leapt up the stairs right behind her and stood between the guardian dogs as she knocked. They were definitely the same statues. I recognized chips and cracks from when I'd seen them in Nagasaki, plus some new scars they must have gotten during the years in between.

Me, too, buddies. I thought to myself, *me, too.*

Inside, Sensei's cheerful voice called, "Who forgot something?" The door opened and Sensei's face appeared. It looked almost identical to the face we had left in Nagasaki only a few hours before. He stopped, surprised, then his smile got even bigger.

"Oh," he said, looking us each in the eye. "It's very good to see you both again."

CHAPTER 22

Sensei ushered us in through the herb room. It smelled just as it had in Nagasaki, and felt very much like it, too. I noticed small changes, though. Some wooden crates were now clear plastic tubs, and I recognized herbs from Brazil and Romania that hadn't been there in the past.

It was like that in the main training space, too: just the same, with updates or changes here and there that somehow underlined the sameness rather than taking away from it. I felt part of me relax deeply just by breathing the air in this space. Other than Mom, it was the thing in the world most like home to me.

We sat at the low table, a different table made of lighter-colored wood, but also the same table in every way that mattered. Sensei brought us tea, going through the same motions as he had in the past. His movements were even more precise and confident than they had been then. I guess more than seventy years of practice will do that.

He closed his eyes, sipped deeply, then set down his cup. When he opened his eyes, I said, "So, it worked? You survived?"

"Yes, *Chuugi*," he said. His voice was just the same as it would have been if I hadn't asked a super-obvious question.

"How? What did we do to save you?"

Sensei paused then, closing his eyes in concentration. Alex shot me a glance, not speaking. Eventually, he opened his eyes and said, "I cannot remember. But I remember another time where I died. To be honest, I prefer this one."

He smiled, and that was all it took. Alex and I couldn't help ourselves. We laughed, then laughed harder, and still harder until my stomach and ribs ached from it and tears streamed down my face in wet, salty sheets. It took a long time to get back under control, but when I did, I felt rested and refreshed like I had just taken a really good nap.

"Sensei," I said, after I had finally recovered.

"Yes?"

"How many of me have you known? How many *Chuugis*?"

Sensei was silent for a long breath. When he spoke, his voice was not intense, but focused. It carried the weight of how important his words were to him. "First, understand that you are the only Connor Morgan in the world. You are yourself, and nobody else is capable of that."

"Besides," Alex said, "who'd want the job?" I laughed, but Sensei continued as if she hadn't interrupted.

"But that's not what you are asking. You want to know that I have met and fought beside five *Chuugis* in my time as Sensei, and two others in my time before that."

Seven of me. I wanted to know how long Sensei had been alive, how long each of them had lived, but more than that I needed to know one thing. "How many....how many went bad?"

"Only one. Only him. Only during the war. *Chuugi*, Loyalty is a difficult value to twist into evil. But when it happens, it creates one of the most powerful of fallen warriors."

A pain very different from the ache from too much laughter ripped through my stomach. I didn't want to know the answer to what I was about to ask, but had to ask it anyway. "Why? What about the others?"

"Every virtue can be twisted around. Wisdom can become arrogance. Courage, recklessness. Even compassion, if warped, can leave one open to manipulation by evil wearing a kind face."

He named each value in the Bushido Code, each of my friends. I imagined them one by one doing terrible things with their power, all thinking they were doing the world a favor.

"So, *Chuugi* and *Jin*," Sensei said, "we must guard not just the world, but ourselves. We must stay vigilant. You know I've seen the consequences of making that mistake."

"But how, Sensei? How do we stop from becoming like the other *Chuugi*, like... Youta?"

"Love, *Chuugi*." Sensei said, still smiling. "Love. If you make your love bigger than your fear, bigger than your pain. If you make it bigger than doubt, and greed, and pride, and even bigger than your mission, it will not steer you wrong."

I thought of Mom. She was the constant best thing in my life, even though we shared some terrible and terrifying memories. I knew she worried, and that I sometimes challenged her patience, but she was always kind with me. She always found a way. Maybe it was because she made love bigger than those things.

Sensei stood, smoothly, and fetched blankets from a small chest beneath a bench. "Sleep on that, *Chuugi*. You are tired, and still have a long fight ahead of you." I wanted to object, but my eyes suddenly felt heavier than...well, um...something very, very heavy. I lay down and used my arm for a pillow.

I started drifting to sleep almost immediately, but I heard Sensei's voice floating in the air. "He knows?"

Alex's voice joined his, "I think so. He may not know he knows."

"Kanashi," Sensei said, in a whisper.

I tried to remember what little Japanese I knew, but their voices of comfort and love sang me to sleep.

CHAPTER 23

A spicy smell wafting through the air woke me up. I felt sore like I'd just done a conditioning session early in the season, but more rested than I had been in years. I rolled over, groaning with the aches, to see Sensei and Alex moving through a slow tai chi form out on the mat.

With his back to me, never turning, Sensei said, "*Chuugi*, welcome back. Come, join us."

Even though I felt like the Tin Man before his daily oil, I got to my feet. Sensei was loving, gentle, and kind, but you did not refuse his invitation to train. By the time

I got to the mat, he and Alex had returned to its center. They stood there, relaxed and sweating lightly.

Sensei nodded to Alex. "*Chuugi*, let's start with a simple Qigong wake-up."

I got into position behind them, just out of reach of Alex's feet. She led us first through raising our arms and lowering them while we breathed deeply in and out. It hurt at first, but my body warmed up and loosened even during the first sequence. We moved through swinging our arms, to circling our arms in a heart shape, and through another fourteen simple, smooth, flowing motions. By the end, we'd performed each movement dozens of times. I felt energized, relaxed, and alert. My muscles didn't hurt anymore, though there was a warm, deep fatigue I could tell wasn't going away any time soon.

Alex turned to me, a small smile on her face. "*Chuugi*, how do you feel?"

"Good. Better than I should, and...hungry."

"Hungry?"

"No. Starving."

"That is fortunate," Sensei said. "Sit, sit."

We ate white rice and small, salty fish together, nobody speaking. Instead, we focused on the taste, smell, and texture of each bite. They ate slower than I usually did, but I changed my pace to match theirs. The food tasted different that way, not exactly better, but richer, and I was full much sooner than I thought I would be. Alex and Sensei finished with a smack of their lips and a pair of smiles that looked very much alike.

Sensei wiped his lips on a worn but clean napkin, then said, "Alex told me what you need, but not how you will get it."

My mouth, operating a little ahead of my brain, said, "I need to go to school."

Four sets of eyebrows raised in surprise. Both of their voices asked, "Why?"

I was surprised to realize I did know why. "There's something on the tip of my brain. Something from what I read or saw last fall. I know what book I saw it in, or at least what it looks like, and I know where it is in the library."

They looked at each other, their surprise mirroring one another. After a while, Sensei said, "All right, then. That is good news." Alex said, "I'll get the car."

"You'll get the what?" I asked, but she was already out of the room.

I followed her to the street, where she was opening an older Toyota with four doors and dull blue paint. I slid into the passenger seat after pulling the adjuster to make room. I strapped in and said, "How did you get a car?"

"Better you don't ask."

As we slipped through the morning traffic, Alex said, "Do you really know what you're going to do when you get there?"

"Sort of," I said. "I know I need to go to the library, and I know that I'll see something that reminds me of another thing, and once I see that thing...I think I'll have a plan."

"Sounds sketchy," Alex said, her voice again sounding like my teenaged friend more than an ancient mentor of warriors.

"Sketchier than running through half a dozen time streams just to take a vacation?"

"You raise a fair point."

As we rounded the corner that lead to Ponderosa High, I had a second of panic when I saw the parking lot full of cars, but no people. That's what Ponderosa looks like when you're running late. I mean, I was late for the start of school, but I wasn't actually supposed to be there at all. Beside me, Alex laughed as she turned into the lot.

"You saw that?"

"I'm a sensei. I see everything."

"Didn't see a solution to our problem yet, though, did you, Sensei?"

"*Touché*, smart ass," she said. She slowed down by the rear entry doors, just long enough to let me out. I slipped through into the empty halls just as the passing bell rang.

It wasn't hard to stay unnoticed in the crowded halls. I belonged there, and nobody who recognized me knew to think it was weird. I felt a weird catch in my stomach as I passed in front of Principal Graff, the same kind I'd feel in the car if there were police behind us whether or not their lights were flashing. But she didn't know what was happening any more than the students around me. She barely gave me a glance as I slid by.

Not too long ago, I'd helped beat her into unconsciousness because we thought she was possessed by an elder demon. It turned out we were wrong, that she was just overcome by *oni* and the crushing pressure of a job as difficult and thankless as hers. Luckily, the experience had left her unable to clearly remember much from the weeks she had been in their power, including how she'd been freed.

The passing bell rang, and the crowd began to thin out. Ahead of me, I saw myself. I was walking hand in hand with Susan, wearing loose jeans and a plain black T-shirt, and headed straight for me. I slipped into a usually empty office Fiel and Galhardo had shown to me once, where they would shelter when they wanted to skip class. I closed the door, breathing a deep sigh of relief.

Behind me, Fiel's voice said, "Nice threads."

I absolutely did not squeak like a frightened mouse at the sound of his voice. I turned around in a calm and collected fashion to find both the brothers standing there holding their phones. I tried to remember what they were avoiding, but maybe they hadn't told me. They both stood there, staring at me.

"Uh, earth to Connor," Fiel said. Galhardo looked up at his twin brother, shaking his head in mock worry. "He's not here."

Fiel said, "Connor, buddy? You okay?" I just looked at them.

Galhardo looked me up and down, one eyebrow arched in curiosity. He practiced that eyebrow arch in the mirror, I knew, but he would never admit it. "Connor....oooooh, Connor?"

"Hey guys," I finally made my mouth move. "What's up?"

They gave me level stares, apparently silenced by the lameness of my response.

"Okay, dude," said Fiel slowly. Galhardo drawled, "you do you." They slipped out the door, moving with exaggerated slowness like they were afraid I'd snap and attack them.

I figured I was safe to move when the sound in the halls died, so I slipped out and walked through the echoing school to the library. It's always weird being in a high school's empty hallways, especially in the middle of the day. They're built to be full of people, and even though they're crowded between classes they feel much too big when you're in them all alone. They reminded me of the empty streets of Nagasaki, another space that needed people to make it feel complete.

Mr. Grubisek, is a bald war veteran so big he made me look average sized, who we of course called Conan the Librarian. He looked down at me from his seat at the circulation desk. "Hey Connor, spill your lunch?"

"Huh?" I said, looking up at him.

He pointed one thumb in my direction, "New threads."

Right. I was wearing the sweats Alex had given me the night before, but the other me had jeans and a t-shirt. "Yeah," I said. "Good thing I had spares in my locker."

He smiled at me the way adults sometimes smile when a kid is being a little weird, but not so weird it's their problem. "Can I help you with something today?"

"No, thank you. I need to look something up, but I know where."

"Then don't let me stop you." He picked up a paperback with the name Robert B. Parker on it, moving his huge finger along as he read.

I let my feet lead me between two long shelves that looked mostly like all the others. They stopped in front of a section of books about Japan. I scanned them until my eyes fell on a text I'd used for a history report early last semester: *An Illustrated Treasury of Japan*. I knew it was the one, even if I couldn't have told anybody why I knew that.

I took the book to one of the study desks in the back, out of sight of the library door, and paged through it. There was a chapter of paintings of ghosts, but that wasn't right. Another chapter on the mythical creatures of Japan. I passed it by, then stopped, paging back to a picture of a badger with enormous feet. The caption said *Tanuki*. I read the paragraph beneath it.

The tanuki racoon dog of Japan is a real animal, one of the earliest extant ancestors of dogs worldwide. The world also refers to a mythological mischief spirit that can take eight different forms, all of which have an enormous scrotum (as large as eight tatami mats, or 130 square feet) and testicles it will use to parachute from the sky, spin to cause fierce winds, or smother hapless victims by covering their faces.

"Wait, what?" I said. I re-read the passage, then re-re-read it. A lot of things made more sense than they had a minute earlier, but I really, really wished they didn't. My imagination filled with the image of a *tanuki* covering my face with what Alex had told me weren't its feet.

"Gaaaghk!" I shouted.

"Mr. Morgan?" Mr. Grubisek called out.

"I'm fine! Sorry!"

He didn't respond, but I heard him turn a page in his book. I'd have to talk to Alex about this later, but for now I turned my own pages, still looking for...I wasn't sure yet. I paged past drawings from history so old it was probably legend, photos from the time of our Civil War, images of the first automobiles to roll through Tokyo's streets, and then there it was.

I'd almost talked, back in the past, about some things I knew about the atomic bombings from my work on a report. I'd used this book, and found the page I was looking at. There, in a photo about the size of a postcard, stood Emperor Hirohito in his black robes. Beside him stood three other men. One of them, to his left, looked familiar, but I still couldn't tell exactly why. I scanned the caption. It was the only known photo taken from the meeting where the sneak attack on Pearl Harbor was planned. The caption labeled the Emperor, Admiral Yamamoto, and General Hideki Tojo, but only said "Unknown" for the fourth man in the picture.

This was it, the thing that had been tickling my brain. I'd seen that unknown person before. He was short by today's standards, but larger than the men around him, and muscular, with a short buzz haircut and eyes that did...something. I couldn't tell what, until suddenly I could.

He looked just like the other *Chuugi*. He *was* the other *Chuugi*. He had been at the meeting where Japan decided to go to war with the United States, a meeting that had ended with two atomic bombs destroying their cities. But how could a Bushido Warrior be a part of something like that? I would never. I could never.

Then it hit me. I could never do that kind of thing if I was still myself, but I remember how I felt when the *oni* had gotten inside of me. I was ready to commit murder, to hurt people who didn't deserve it, because I was no longer myself. If Mrs. Dochevnya hadn't saved me, if I had fallen all the way, I absolutely could do something like that.

The *Chuugi* of that time, the *Chuugi* who had seen all six of his brother and sister warriors killed, had fallen. He had fallen and made a disastrous war so much worse by somehow gaining the ears of the Emperor and his two most trusted military leaders, and convincing them to attack the United States.

And he was there with Sensei right now, the only person giving my mentor advice that could save or end his life.

"Gaaaghk!" I shouted again.

Mr. Grubicek's voice boomed through the stacks, "Mr. Morgan, you are aware this is a library?"

I stood up, leaving the book open on the table behind me, and stumbled out into the halls. "Sorry, Mr. Grubicek. I have to...I have to..." and I joined the flow of my classmates. I let them carry me while my mind whirled, a small part of me keeping an eye out for myself. I didn't see me, and I narrowly avoided young Alex by ducking behind a support pillar and turning to walk the other way.

I headed toward the rear doors by the locker rooms, where Alex would be to pick me up soon. At the main intersection, I saw Coach Fagin and Mr. Waldron talking. Coach looked bored, maybe even annoyed. Mr. Waldron looked like he was telling some kind of story. His mouth opened wide and he moved his hands in sharp, chopping gestures.

Then I saw it. Mr. Waldron looked like *Chuugi* because he was *Chuugi*. He was still alive, and younger-looking, for the same reason that Sensei hadn't aged more than a few years in seven decades. I steered around them, turning my face away but wondering what would happen if I took him out then and there. Would it stop the war? Would it save Sensei in the past, or seal us into this new timeline where he died long ago? Would I die in a few days? What would the police have to say if I assaulted a teacher with no warning?

And I couldn't give him any warning. He was me, with my strength and magical powers, and a hundred years to practice them. If I took him out, if that would even work, it would have to be by surprise with no warning. It would have to be murder. Even if I saved my life and Sensei's, it would kill Mom to see me go to jail like my dad.

It was too much for me. I would have to ask Alex. I watched Mr. Waldron out of the corner of my eye as I turned a corner and walked right into Susan.

CHAPTER 24

"Hey there, gorgeous," said Susan. My brain did a kind of mental hiccup as I tried to change gears from plotting the possible murder of a hundred-year old fallen Bushido Warrior to chatting with my gorgeous girlfriend.

"Nice threads," said Tosha, who was standing next to her. "*Tres chic.*"

Susan said, "Yeah. Babe, what happened to your jeans and t-shirt?"

"Did you two soil his clothing and not tell me about it?" Tosha said, sticking out her tongue and giving me a thumbs up.

I couldn't think of anything to say. My brain was still hiccupping and I was still processing too much information all at once, so I kissed her. I really kissed her, the way you do when nothing in the world exists but you and the person you're kissing. As she melted into the kiss and started to return it, pretty much it was that way for me, too.

Susan wrapped her arms around my neck and kissed me back. She tasted like Jolly Rancher candy and her hair smelled like chocolate.

"Woah, there," Tosha said from someplace very far away. "If you don't plan to tag a girl in, I'm going to need you to slow things down guys."

We ignored her. We had better things to pay attention to.

The bell rang. I could barely hear it, and most of me didn't want to understand what it meant, but Susan broke the kiss and pulled away. She looked at me through her eyelashes. "To be continued?"

"Yes," I said, my voice very hoarse for some reason. I wondered if the other me would keep my promise for me.

Susan and Tosha went their way. I went mine, through the halls, past the locker rooms, out the door and into the car waiting in the pickup lane. Alex drove us over the speed bumps and onto the main road.

"Seriously, though, Alex. Did you steal this?"

"No."

"Really?"

"Well. Not really. When we fix everything, we'll have never been here. I will never have taken the car, so the owner won't ever have had their car stolen. No harm, no foul, right?"

"So you did steal it."

"No!"

"But you took it without asking. How do you know how to do that?"

"I don't. The sonic screwdriver does. Did you find out what you needed to know?" She turned off the main road, into a city park I'd never visited before. The trees were darker and thicker than most of the ones I was used to here in Portland, more like the wilder spaces in Eugene or further south.

"Yes," I said, then I told her what I'd found out about *Chuugi* and Mr. Waldron, and about how I'd thought about murdering him there in the middle of the hall.

"It's probably best you didn't do that," Alex said as she pulled into a parking spot. She looked at me with the focused intensity our Sensei sometimes got. "We don't know what it would do to the space-time continuum, but I'm pretty sure I know what it would have done to you." She stared at me until I got it.

I remembered what I'd thought about the earlier *Chuugi*, and how I'd felt when the demons got into my head. "I...if I murdered him in cold blood, I would stop being me, and..."

"I think so. We'd just replace that fallen Bushido Warrior with a fresh, new model." She poked at her sonic screwdriver and hopped out of the car. "So, I'm, uh, really glad you didn't do that."

I jumped out and followed her down a bare dirt path, up a hill and around the corner to a clearing filled with the throbbing purple light of a gate already forming.

"We cut it close," I said to Alex. "Are you sure you know what you're doing?"

"Not even a little bit. But nobody else wants the job."

We looked at each other then, with the light growing brighter. I could have wished for more of our friends with us then, to help us complete our mission, but there was nobody in the world I would rather face it with. I smiled at my friend.

"Let's do the thing," she said.

I nodded, and led the way.

CHAPTER 25

"Crap," Alex said. Her voice penetrated the fog of pain and disorientation from the jump.

"What?" I asked. I breathed out the last mental fog to see her looking at the sonic screwdriver, face wrinkled with concern. We were in a bunch of trees, but not the park next to the dojo. These trees were thick, tall, untended and choked with underbrush. We were deep in the woods.

"Super duper mega super crap," Alex said.

"What?" I repeated. But she was already striding down a path between the trees as quickly as her shorter legs would take her. My own legs felt like jelly as I jogged to catch up. "What?"

"I miscalculated. We're further from the dojo than I expected. Long way to go. Short time to get there."

"That's from something, isn't it? Was it a song?" I asked as we half-ran, half-walked through the trees. The path under my feet was soft dirt, coated with dead leaves. It was smooth, and no roots tripped us as we moved.

"It'll be from our obituaries if we don't hustle."

"Okay," I said. I don't have many talents, but hustling is one of them even when I'm tired. Even when I'm as exhausted as I've ever been. When it comes to putting my head down and moving one foot in front of the other, I am world class.

So we hustled.

We ran fast and loud through the woods, down a muddy slope, through air strangely thick with humidity despite the winter chill, and into the streets of Nagasaki. When we reached the cobbled roads, we jogged slower and more quietly to the park. To my surprise, nothing saw, chased, stopped, or tried to kill us the whole way.

Then we broke out of the park and saw a whole lot of *oni* doing all four, only not to us.

Well, yes to us. But not to *us* us. To the other us.

In the alley next to the dojo, Alex-Sensei and I were surrounded by *oni*. Demons of all shapes roiled around us, while a troop of *tanuki* dropped on us from the eaves. I heard myself say, "Gah! It choked me with its feet!"

"Not its feet!" that Alex shouted back, as the *oni* closed to battle.

The chittering swarm advanced on them...um, on us...um, on the other us. They surged to just outside of kicking range. I said, "We should help us."

"Why?" Alex said. It wasn't really a question. "We know we make it."

A small, turtle-shaped demon broke ranks and charged. Alex kicked it so hard it passed through three other demons. They all dissipated into greasy smoke.

"Hmm," I said. "This is weird. Nice kick, though."

"Yes," said Alex. "This is really, really weird. And thanks. I remember being pretty proud of it."

We watched the scene unfold, our fight against the swarm of little demons until One-Arm and his cruel troop interrupted us just in time to get possessed by all the surviving *oni*. Then *Chuugi*...um, the other *Chuugi* came and drove them away. He spoke quickly with One-Arm and we had to hide while the soldiers walked past us into the park. Our doubles followed Sensei inside.

From my place in the shadows, I whispered to Alex. "I know what they are."

"What, uh, what who are?" Alex asked. Her eyes never left the dojo door.

"The tansockies."

"You mean the *tanukis*?"

"Yeah."

"And what is it you think you know about them?" Even though she was facing the dojo, I could see the high arched eyebrows of her expression in my mind's eye. Some things never change in people, no matter how much weird stuff happens to them.

"They aren't feet."

"I remember telling you exactly as much," Alex said. Her voice quavered slightly.

"I know what they are."

She kept silent, smiling now. I stared her down, or tried to. It was like staring down a cat. Almost like a purr, she sang a tune under her breath.

Tan tan tanuuki no kintama wa
Kaze mo nai no ni bura bura
Sore wo mite ita oya danuki
Onaka wo kakaete wahha haha

She was still singing quietly when we left the dojo, walking with *Chuugi*. I watched them stop at the edge of the park, heard that Alex's voice over the rustle of the wind.

"He'll die!"

"It is not for you to decide," *Chuugi* shot back. After a few more words, he turned on his heel and stormed toward the dojo. The wind picked up and that pair of us melted into the shadows of the park. And then something weird happened.

The shadows in the alleys all around coalesced into dozens of *oni*. They chittered with wicked excitement, but they didn't attack. They didn't seem to even notice us. Instead, they ran right past us, jumping like puppies, to roil over and around the other *Chuugi*. They formed a cloud of darkness all around him as he walked away, down the road and into the night. If I'd had any doubts about what I'd seen in the library, they were gone now.

Chuugi had turned, and he had convinced Sensei to stay in Nagasaki for the bomb only a few hours away.

CHAPTER 26

When the last tread of *Chuugi*'s footsteps faded into the night, Alex glided out of our hiding space and ran three impossibly long steps to leap silently up to the dojo porch. I got there too, but with not nearly as much grace. I reached down and scratched the lion dog statue nearest me behind one ear. I whispered, "Good dog."

"Scratch the other one, too," Alex said.

"What? Why?"

"So he doesn't get jealous."

I grumbled, but shifted over and scratched the other statue behind its curly, stone ear. Alex knocked on the door.

When Sensei opened the door, his face held a moment of confusion, then a trickle of surprise rose from his mouth to his eyes. Then he threw back his head and laughed with pure and obvious joy. This made Alex laugh, too, and I chuckled while I watched the shadows for *oni* or soldiers who might have been attracted by the noise. Some smaller demons were up in the tree, but I flexed my will at them. It surfed on the current of my friends' laughter, and the monsters ran away.

"Ohairi!" Sensei said. "Come in. Come in." His voice still shook gently with amusement like...well, like an old man having a weird night who had just seen something that struck his funny bone. "As it happens, I have tea ready. Do you know why?"

"Yes, Sensei," Alex said. We followed him through the herb room and into the dojo. It was just as we had left it, with the tea still out and steaming at the table. Which made sense, since we had just left it minutes before even though days had passed for both of us.

As he sat at the tea table, Sensei asked Alex, "You understand why I asked?"

"Yes," Alex said.

"No," I said. I was still trying to figure out the first question.

"Connor," Alex said. Her voice was gentle and kind, even though she was still laughing with Sensei. "He doesn't know yet which time stream you and I are part of."

I still wasn't sure I understood completely, but I felt like that most days of my life. I let it go, and sat down with them at the table. Our tea steamed in the delicate, beautiful bowls. Sensei topped off our cups.

He sat and sipped, his eyes closed and his face relaxing into a blank serenity as he swallowed. Then he opened his eyes and looked at us with his gentle smile. "So. You are here to change my mind, as you have already experienced our recent conversations?"

"Yes, Sensei," I said.

"Why do you think my mind has changed, that *Chuugi's* — this time's *Chuugi's* — mind has changed. It has been less than one hundred breaths since you came."

"We are here to change your mind," Alex said.

"But my mind will not change," Sensei's face still wore his serene smile, but there was a stony determination behind it. He wasn't being stubborn, but he had made up his mind. It would take a lot to change it.

"You must come with us," Alex said. "Her voice was thick with worry. "You must leave Nagasaki. Tonight. You will die if you remain."

Sensei's face grew stern. "Selfishness and ego are where the corruption of a Bushido Warrior begins. If you are correct about the second bomb, it is a catastrophe, but a hidden blessing. The Emperor cannot possibly continue the war if the Americans can drop such bombs forever. But so much death and loss is too much. Too much..."

"And you can't be among those dead," Alex said, tears dripping down her face. I felt my own eyes grow hot from seeing such pain in my mentor. "Think what the *oni* could do without you to fight them. You must come with us, out of this city, to where you can be safe."

"I cannot," Sensei said, his voice rough with sorrow. "Now, please leave. I must make my preparations."

"Miyamoto-Sensei," Alex said. Her voice was as firm as our teacher's. "Your preparations will come to naught."

"That may be so," Sensei returned.

"It *will* be so!" Alex shouted. I jumped a little, sloshing my tea into my lap. Alex never shouted, and this wasn't even Alex-Alex. This was Alex-Sensei, who probably shouted less. If the lapse bothered Sensei, he didn't show it.

"It may be so, and I will not abandon my city to fire and death. Even if it means dying with them."

"Instead of living among the survivors, where you can be of help?" Alex said. "Her voice had calmed, but I could see the fear and frustration in the way her arms vibrated as she spoke. "Are you so eager to put down your burden that you would abandon them when they need you more than anybody has ever needed you?"

"*Jubun'na!*" This time, it was Sensei shouting. Some of the anger I had seen earlier flashed across his face, then he grew calm again like a pond after a rock falls into it. The ripples were gone before he spoke again. "I cannot decide to flee this fight. I am not important enough to be saved. None of us are. Not you. Not I. Not the *Chuugi* of my time. Not the *Chuugi* here with us now. No one of us can believe we are more important than the burdens we carry. Not one of our lives is greater or dearer than the least of the lives we protect."

Sensei stared at Alex, and she returned his gaze. Though neither of them spoke, the energy between them was so intense I felt like I could hear it. I didn't want to say anything, to get in between these two people who knew so much more than I did, but I knew something they weren't considering.

"Sensei," I said. My voice was higher and tighter than I usually liked it. "What if I said you were getting bad advice?"

"Wait, what?" Alex said. She looked annoyed for a split second before she visibly relaxed. Sensei was silent, but gave me a look that said the same thing, only in 1940s Japanese.

"Sensei, what if somebody you trusted was lying to you? What if that person had convinced you to stay here even though it would lose the Bushido War?"

Sensei looked shocked. It might have been the first time I'd seen that emotion in him, ever. "But," he said. "But, who would do such a thing?"

The door opened then, and in walked *Chuugi*.

CHAPTER 27

"Speak of the devil," Alex said. Sensei looked at her confused, like she'd used a saying he wasn't used to. Actually, that was exactly it.

"You!" *Chuugi* shouted. He stormed into the dojo, hand on his katana.

"*Dame!*" Sensei called out, one hand up with his palm toward the warrior. *Chuugi* stopped, but his focus and intent went past our master with so much power it felt like it could cut me all by itself.

"Sensei," I started, my voice shaking.

"Do not speak to him!" *Chuugi*'s voice rattled the walls.

Sensei looked surprised. "*Chuugi*, he said. These are our guests, our brother and sister who have traveled farther than anybody we have ever met."

"They are clouding your vision, *Sensei*. They want you to leave this place, where you are needed most!"

"No," Alex said. "We want you to leave this place where you are going to die!"

"Liar!" *Chuugi* shouted.

I don't know what made me say it, but I put on a singsong, kid voice and said, "I know you are, but what am I?"

Everybody stared at me, each of their faces showing different kinds of surprise and confusion. Apparently, Sensei and *Chuugi* didn't know that saying either. I carried on before I could lose my nerve. "You're the liar, *Chuugi*. You started this war, betrayed Bushido. How many of the other warriors did you kill?"

Chuugi's hand went to his katana. In the fraction of a second between his beginning to draw and the metal of his blade showing from the sheath, Sensei shouted *"Dame!"* with such force and authority all three of us froze like statues.

The silence after Sensei's word felt physical. It curdled like bad milk in the air between everybody as they all stared at me. I felt very small and very afraid, but also very angry. How could *Chuugi* betray everything we stood and fought for? Yes, I had been possessed by demons and knew how it felt, but I had overcome it. This *Chuugi* was bigger, older, and more powerful than me. Why hadn't he fought more?

I said, clearly and carefully. "*Chuugi* helped start the war. He was in the room in January, with Yamamoto and Hirohito and all the others, when they decided to attack Pearl Harbor. I saw the pictures."

They all kept staring, saying nothing. Sensei and *Chuugi*'s expressions didn't change. Sensei's stayed impassive and curious, while *Chuugi*'s was a mask of barely contained rage. Alex cocked her head and raised an eyebrow.

"I don't know when you fell, *Chuugi*," I said to the man in front of me, his hand still on his sword. "But you fell. You helped create this war, and it's going to mean tens of thousands die right here, in just a few hours."

Alex said, "You can't change that. But you can help with what happens next. Come home, *Chuugi*."

Chuugi's face didn't change. His knuckles grew whiter in their grip on the katana's handle. The tiniest gleam of metal showed between its guard and the sheath. I shifted my weight, getting ready to spring if any more metal appeared.

Alex said again, "Come home."

The giant warrior didn't move, but somehow seemed smaller. It was like when my father would start sobering up, the anger leaving him to expose the fear and sadness hiding behind its mask. The glint of metal disappeared as the blade slid back into its scabbard.

Alex's face creased in concentration, her focus on him something I could physically feel. "*Chuugi*," she said, quietly. Then, as her face smoothed with some kind of realization, she named him again. "*Chuugi*. Masaharu. Maza."

Sensei's voice cut in, "*Chuugi*, you said you were helping refugees."

Chuugi's face finally changed. For the briefest instant, the anger and resolve carried a shadow of shame, but only for an instant.

"I was helping," his voice was small.

Sensei just looked at him, the way Mom would look at me when I still would lie to her, and she was disappointed about it. Silence stretched between them until Sensei said, his face stretched tight like a mask made for a much smaller man, "*Chuugi*, this can't be so."

All the doubt fell off *Chuugi's* face like stones in an avalanche. The rage returned, twisting his mouth and his words. "You stupid old man! *Damare konoyarou!*"

Sensei flinched. I didn't know what the words meant, but I could tell they were the sort of thing Mom would be disappointed in me for saying at all, let alone to somebody like Sensei. *Chuugi* stared at us all, one hand on the pommel of each of his swords. It seemed for a moment like the air was turning red from his anger alone, then I realized it wasn't the air. It was the lantern with our symbol, the symbol *Chuugi*, of loyalty. Its flame had turned crimson and was burning so hot the lantern itself was beginning to glow.

Chuugi's breath was like a train engine, bellowing in and out of him as he boiled in his rage. Sensei's face went slack with horror and I knew he knew. We all knew it. *Chuugi* knew. For a fraction of a second, another emotion passed over his face, something childlike, and frightened, and ashamed, but the mask of anger slammed down over it. Whether it crushed it or just hit it, I couldn't tell.

A crack like a gunshot split the air of the room at the same instant a thunderclap sounded in the air all around us. On the shelf beside us, his lantern, my lantern, burst into shards.

"*Taihen da*," Sensei said. He looked at *Chuugi*, both of them standing as still as the dog statues just outside the door. The air rang with silence.

Chuugi said nothing else. He snorted, like a horse with a cold, and shook his head. Then he stalked out of the dojo. A second later, the door crashed as he kicked or just walked through it.

Sensei dropped to his knees. He looked so sad, so broken in that moment I didn't have the heart to say anything.

Alex said, gently, "Now will you come with us?"

Sensei stood, his face stricken. "No. No, I will not. This changes nothing. Now, please leave a tired old man with much work left to do." He shuffled, slowly, like his entire being hurt, to the shards of the lantern. He tried to piece them together like a jigsaw puzzle.

"Sensei?" I said. He didn't answer. In Alex's pocket, her sonic screwdriver chimed.

"Sensei?" I said again. He paused in his efforts, but didn't answer or turn around. He just held the pieces, testing the edges against one another with hands clumsier than I had ever seen from him.

The sonic screwdriver chimed again. Alex took my arm. "*Chuugi*, we have to go."

I looked at my mentor, my heart hurting for him. For the first time in my life, I thought I understood what it was like for Mom to see me injured. What it would be like for Mom to see me die.

"*Chuugi*," Alex said again. "It's time to go."

"So that's it, then?" I asked. She pulled on my arm and I turned my back on Sensei, leaving him to his grief.

"No," she said. "There's one last ripple."

CHAPTER 28

We slunk outside together, each of us petting one of the dogs' heads as we went. The street was empty, so we slipped back into the park and out the other side. We both were silent as we moved, lost in our thoughts. I was so sad and scared for Sensei I couldn't think of anything else. I wasn't inside Alex's head, but I imagined she was feeling pretty similar.

She led me down a street we hadn't taken yet, running through tightly locked wooden buildings. No light shone inside, but I heard once in a while the sound of a whispered voice, or something set down harder than it should have been. The street turned from cobblestones, to wooden slats, to rock, to a dirt track as the homes thinned out and the trees grew thicker. Soon, we were running on a narrow track through the jungle, up a hill and out of town.

Halfway up a steep slope walled in and roofed by thick trees, Alex stopped in her tracks. She put her hands on her knees and breathed in a weird but controlled pattern. Between inhales, she gasped, "I'm...old...*Chuugi*...deal...with...it."

I put one hand on her hip and the other on her shoulder, helping her stand upright. Bending over like that collapses the bottom half of your lungs, and makes it harder to catch your breath. My friend leaned into my arm, and I gladly took her weight. We waited together in the dark, smelling the POW camp on the wind. As her breath returned to normal, I asked her.

"Hey, Alex-Sensei?"

"Yes, *Chuugi*?" her voice had returned to mostly normal, but I could tell by how hard she leaned on me that she was still hurting.

"What happens to us if Sensei dies in the morning?"

"Remember that time I told you nobody really understands how time travel works?" Alex pulled away from me with a nod of thanks, and started down the leaf-covered path. I followed.

"Yeah. I remember that."

"Keep that in mind, but here's what smart people think. They believe time works in one of three ways. One is *sticky time*, where you can go back and change small things, but the big picture works out the same. We could go back and kill Hitler, but some guy named Hans would rise to power and do all the same bad stuff."

"Okay," I said. I actually understood that.

"So if that's the case, then not much will happen to the Bushido War. But it's anybody's guess what happens to you and me. It's just as likely we'll die somehow, and be replaced in the future by some other kids."

I ducked under a low-hanging branch, wincing. These were not comforting thoughts. Alex said, "With me so far?" and I told her yes.

"Okay. Next you have *free flowing time*, where history is fragile and things change easily. Like in that Ray Bradbury story."

"What Ray Bradbury story."

"*The Sound of Thunder*. Some people go back in time and accidentally kill a butterfly, and the whole world has changed when they get back. If that's the truth, this could make us lose the Bushido War forever because there's nothing to prevent all the changes Sensei's death here would cause."

"That would....that would be bad," I said. My mind spun a little about how many things Sensei's absence would have meant for my life alone, and I'd only known him for a few months. "How likely is that?"

"Nobody knows. That's the thing with time magic. Last, you have *parallel universes*. That says if you change time, it creates two different realities. In one, the change happens. In the other, it didn't."

"I think I like that one the least," I said. We slowed our pace to climb an even steeper hill. I crossed to the front so I could offer Alex my hand to help. She ignored it, but asked me why.

"That one leaves a universe where Mom sees me die. I don't want that in any universe."

When we reached the top, Alex stopped, gulping in lungfuls of air. When she could, she said, "Then we'd better figure out a way to not let that universe happen." We stood together at the top of the hill, on a ridge overlooking the dim lights of the POW camp. Even in the dark, I could sense the pain, desperation, and squalor of the men imprisoned there. It was like a bad smell, only inside my mind.

That happened with *oni* and sound sometimes. They would scream in a way that passed my ears and went straight into my brain. It was creepy. This was worse. The concentrated misery of the prison below us changed the air, physically and psychically...and must have been making all the *oni* hanging out there as fat and happy as a demon could hope for.

And I'd thought high school gave them an all-you-can-eat buffet.

"Most of them came through Bataan," Alex said quietly. She stood beside me while the wind drew the stench of the camp toward us. "Soldiers captured in the Philippines were marched to ships, then brought here in conditions I don't know how to describe. More than two thousand died before they got here, and more down there after they did."

I had nothing to say about that. I couldn't think of any words that wouldn't feel small and petty next to the size of it.

After a while, Alex said, "Did you know Fiel and Galhardo's grandfather learned jujitsu from a man who took his first lessons at a camp like this? They gave him an extra helping of rice for his daily food if he let them use him as a training dummy."

"And he survived to teach?"

"He did."

"How?"

Alex leaned against me, her shoulder pressing against my elbow. "I have no idea, *Chuugi*. But that's what we do, isn't it?"

"Who, us?"

"Well, us, too. But people. It's amazing what people will survive, and recover from, with enough time."

"But how?" I asked. I'd been through some things, but they all felt so small compared to what the men below had gone through. To the sorrow Sensei was feeling just a few miles away. To Mom's pain if we failed and I died after all.

"Ask me again later," she said. She pointed to a dark space that had begun to glow with a purple light. As it grew brighter, I realized we were looking at a cave in a wall of earth and stone. It had been completely invisible in the darkness. "That's our ride."

We approached the cave, which was about the size of my apartment and filled with sacks of stones. People had come here, placing piles of small stones on top of larger stones, making the floor eerie and solemn at the same time.

"Will you look at that?" Alex breathed. She stared at the tiny stacks in rapt attention.

"I know, right?" I said. I was right there with her. The piles were so precise, so perfect. I didn't know how I could walk through them to reach the gate. I didn't know why I would want to. This was a work of art, created collectively over decades or centuries. We had no right to disturb it.

Above the stones, the gate grew to its full size. Its purple light cast them into sharper and even more beautiful relief. I caught a glimpse of stark darkness at its center, and suddenly remembered why we were in this weird cave in the first place.

"Hey, Alex," I said. My friend didn't answer. She just kept staring at the piles of stones. She had a point. They were very, very interesting.

But we had a world to save, and a me to not let tie. I shouted, "Hey! Alex! Time to go!"

She grunted, but didn't move. Her whole attention was on the stones, her whole mind. Maybe her whole soul.

The gate started spinning and flashing, in a way that told me it would close soon. We were out of time, so I did what I would do in that situation with any of my friends. I punched her in the arm. Hard.

"What the? Hey! Ow!" she said. She shook her head and gave me a hurt look, which blossomed to full awareness as she took in the now-shrinking gate. I watched her just long enough to be sure she was with me, then jumped through. A burning line ran across my thighs above and beyond the cramping I'd come to expect. My entire being sneezed, and I landed hard on some tile. I leapt to my feet, reaching toward the gate to physically pull Alex through if I had to.

But the space was already smaller than my head. I could see her, looking tiny and far away. Her hands moved, and a rectangular something grew large in my vision. It passed through the gate, and I caught it with both hands.

I had just enough time to realize it was the sonic screwdriver before the gate closed, leaving Alex behind.

CHAPTER 29

I staggered backward, bumping into some kind of rack, and fell to my knees in the tiny, dark room. Whatever had happened in that cave with those piles of stone, I had failed Alex. Both Alexes. I had failed the Bushido Warriors and the Bushido War. I had failed Susan, and Sensei.

I had failed Mom.

Mom. Did this all mean I was really destined to die at the tournament? That mom would live with that pain for the rest of her life? Just thinking about it made me feel like my brain was going to throw up. I wished and hoped for solutions, like maybe I had jumped back just after my death so I could trick her into thinking I had survived. Would that work? Could it work? What day was it? What time?

The sonic screwdriver beeped. I brought it up and tapped the screen. A passcode panel appeared. I had no idea how to find out what it was trying to tell me.

It beeped again. I said a bad word.

A door opened then, flooding the area with light. When my eyes adjusted, I could see somebody in a janitor outfit. He was short, and thin, with a patch on his coveralls that said ANDRIY.

"Woah," he said. He had an accent, but I couldn't tell from where. "What the hell are you doing in here, kid?"

From the light, I could now tell that *here* was a janitor supply closet. The rack I'd backed into held rows of cleaning supplies, and there was a plastic sink against one wall.

"I'm lost," I said. "I'm here for the wrestling tournament."

"Whatever, kid. I'm calling security. They'll get you where you need to be." He reached for a walkie-talkie clipped into one of his pockets.

"No, seriously. I just need to find the locker rooms."

He paused, his hand resting on the top of his radio. He looked me over, scanned my torn uniform and tired face. I probably looked like a druggie, or somebody who'd raid an unlocked janitor closet for ingredients to make meth or paint to huff. I was going to jail, where I would be trapped with Alex stuck in time and Mom thinking I was dead.

His hand slipped off the walkie-talkie. He said, "Get out of here, you weirdo."

I got out of there, and into the wide corridor that surrounds the arena at Memorial Coliseum. It smelled like nachos, and hot dogs, and I realized how long it had been since I'd really eaten. My stomach didn't growl. It roared.

The sonic screwdriver buzzed again. I pulled it out and stared at the lock screen, trying to think what Alex's code might be. Walking through the crowd, paying more attention to the screwdriver than my surroundings, I must have looked like any random teenager. Not like a warrior who had just failed the entire world, and his best friends, and his Mom along with it.

I was so distracted I literally bumped into Susan. She must have seen me coming, because she sort of molded onto me and turned it into a hug.

"Texting me, I hope?" She pulled out her own phone to look, and frowned when she didn't see the message I hadn't sent her.

"Texting who, then?"

"Nobody," I slipped the sonic screwdriver into my pocket. "I was trying to figure out what time it is."

She flipped her phone so I could see the screen. Above a selfie of us kissing, I could see the time and date. The numbers might have made sense to a smarter person who wasn't completely exhausted and in the middle of a bunch of time travel. Instead, the information just walked through my mind without leaving any footprints.

"Uh, thanks."

"You're welcome." She stood very still in front of me, just out of reach. "What are you doing for the rest of the night?"

"We're going to the dojo. It's kind of like a training camp."

"I thought you said Sensei didn't approve of tournaments, that he said ego wasn't part of your training."

"He does say that, but that doesn't mean he won't help however he can." I said that out loud, but his being at the tournament worried me. Might it have something to do with how I'd died earlier? From what Alex-Sensei had said, he could have felt the change and come to try to stop it from happening.

Susan said, "Are you even listening?" She sounded annoyed.

"What?"

"I just offered you a massage and whatever that might lead to, and you didn't even react. Connor Morgan, that sort of thing could hurt a girl's feelings."

I shook my head, trying to clear the cobwebbed tangle of thoughts. "Sorry. I'm just really tired."

She gave me a hard look, and as she did her own face softened from annoyed to worried. "Yeah. Wow, you are. Look at you, Tiger. Let's get you out of here. Sage just finished her last match and everybody is packing up."

The next hour or so got very fuzzy. Susan and I joined Sage, Alex, Fiel, and Galhardo somewhere else in the hallway. Somehow, we ended up in Alex's blue Subaru, with me in the middle of the back seat. I'm pretty sure Susan kissed me goodnight, but it might have been Alex.

Or Fiel. Then the car was moving, and I was asleep before we got out of the parking garage.

CHAPTER 30

I woke up I don't know how much later, still in the back of Alex's car. My body hurt everywhere, and I felt underwater. My vision was blurry, and my ears stuffed up. I even smelled tired, if that's really a thing.

What was I thinking before about how warriors endure? This warrior wanted a shower, a fistful of Advils, and a week and a quarter of uninterrupted sleep. I couldn't remember the last time I felt so terrible.

I laid back again, groaning, and let my mind drift over the past few days. As I thought of the fights, the running, my matches, and my time in that polluted river, I felt each one as if it freshly happened. All the injuries flared up, seasoned with a tiredness so deep it started at my bones. I'd been awake for days and eaten only a little even with the break Alex had found for us earlier in the week.

And in less than twenty-four hours, Mom would watch me die.

Adrenaline from that thought washed away most of the pain, a lot of the exhaustion, and all of my self-pity. Mom. I had to find a way to stop myself from dying, no matter what it did to the time river thing. I had to find a way to win the war, to rescue Alex from the Future and Sensei from his new, changed past.

I had to figure out when and where I was.

A look out the car window immediately answered the first question. Alex had parked her car across the street from the dojo, directly opposite the stairway leading to the front door. It looked more modern than the dojo in Nagasaki. Concrete stairs instead of cut stone. A door of flat, milled wood instead of carved by hand. The lights were electrical. But Ah and Um had the same scars and chips, plus some new ones. They wore the same expressions on their faces. A feeling emanated from that stoop that was the exact same as what radiated from the one in that other year in that other country. This was home, no matter where and when it was.

As I looked, I swear Um winked at me, like it knew what I knew. But how could it know? It was a statue. I wanted to ask Alex-Sensei about it, but Alex-Sensei wasn't there.

Because she was stuck in the past. I had the sonic screwdriver, which meant I could rescue her. If I could figure out how to use it in time to catch the last gate to 1945. If I couldn't, she might find a way to save Sensei. She probably would. But what would that mean to the decades between then and now? What would happen in her future with Alex-Sensei lost? What would happen to me tomorrow? To Mom?

I had to get back. Which meant using the sonic screwdriver. Which meant I had to unlock it. Which I didn't know how to do.

I reached for the device resting heavy in my pocket. At that moment, Sage came out the dojo door. She was smiling and shouted something I couldn't make out back through the door before it closed. She walked toward me, fierce and strong in the streetlights. Sage Kaiser was a tall, fit, powerful woman and I could see in that moment why Susan was so jealous of her, but I felt nothing for my friend but fond respect. When she saw me awake, she smiled wider and made the window-rolling gesture with one hand.

I obeyed as she closed the last few steps. "She said, "How you holding up, sleepyhead?"

"Like somebody hit me with...with a, well, um, with something you hit people with so they feel totally wiped out."

Sage made a face. "What's up with that? Usually you're the guy who's just getting started when the rest of us gas out."

"Just fatigued," I said. I rubbed my face with the hand that wasn't holding Fiel's device.

Sage looked at me, harder and longer than most people would look at a friend. Slowly, she said, "Everything okay at home, Connor?"

I thought about the letter from our landlord, but this was no time to get into that. I'd need to know Sage could help before asking her to help carry that particular part of my load. "Pretty much," I said. "My matches were just tougher than I expected today."

Sage's face said she didn't quite believe me, but that she knew I was tired. It also promises she wasn't going to let the question go forever. She reached through the window, unlocked the door, and used her other hand to open it. "Let's get you inside. Susan's waiting to take you home. We would have moved you earlier, but you are very large and extremely heavy."

I groaned my way out of the car and followed her across the street, up the stairs, and through the door. Every step sent aches and tingles up my legs and through my back. A body the size of mine is not built for sleeping in the middle seat of commuter hatchbacks.

Ah and Um didn't move as I passed through them, but I felt an energy from them, a light I couldn't quite see. They, like the door and the dojo beyond it, like Mom, felt like home. A home it was my job to protect, if I could just figure out how.

The herb room smelled like it always had. I scanned the shelves, wondering if there might be something to help me get three days' worth of sleep in just a couple of hours. As I looked, I realized they were all labeled in Japanese. I wondered how many boxes, or even how many ingredients, had been in the dojo in Nagasaki. Had I passed by some of these 70 years before? Or was it a few hours? I sat at the table, then lay back to look at the ceiling. I thought about my leg, and the exercises Sensei had taught Alex to help with my recovery. About the weird poultices Avo had put on my leg, how much they stank and how well they worked.

I should have still been on crutches, but instead I was wrestling and winning. I was sprinting across doomed cities in other times. The doctors believed they had misdiagnosed the damage, but Sensei said otherwise. There was some magic in what he, and Avo, and even Alex had done. But I was getting used to magic.

"Come on, buddy," Sage said. She hoisted me back to my feet and pushed me gently into the main dojo room.

It was the weirdest feeling. The dark straw mat and tea table were exactly the same as at the old dojo. Next to them, though, the sumo ring was gone and a boxing ring in its place. Western and eastern weapons hung on the wall racks. Plus the whole place was in Portland, Oregon, in the 21st century and not Nagasaki, Japan in the middle of the 20th.

Even though my eyes must have slid over them I don't know how many times, I kept not really seeing the lanterns. I was nervous about what they might tell me. Would they still glow with that angry red light? Would Alex's be different even though she was there at the table laughing with Galhardo?

Sensei came out of his room then, smiling his peaceful smile. My stomach tingled with a warmth of relief mixed with pangs of worry. Did his being here mean Alex had somehow succeeded in the past, that he had survived the bombing? Or did it mean his death hadn't happened yet in the past? Was he still in danger?

I tried to think it through, to make a plan, but I couldn't. It was too confusing. There was too much I didn't know. I wasn't even sure there was anything I could do. I was so tired the thoughts and facts and ideas slid through my mind like fish in water. If I tried to grab one and do something with it, it would slip through my mind and swim away.

My eyes roamed and my mind raced. I made myself focus on my lantern, the one carved with the same Bushido symbol I'd been born with on my back. It was dark, unlit, just like before...but the wall was cracked along its surface. It looked like a strong wind might blow it apart.

It hadn't had those before. What did that mean? And if I figured out what it meant, what could I do about it?

Through the confusion, I realized something else. Something was happening around me. It took me a few moments to realize I was getting congratulations and applause from my friends. I shook myself out of my own head and waited for the cheers and raspberries to calm down. Then I said, "Hey. Sage won both her matches in the first round. She set a tournament record. Where are her congratulations?"

Susan was standing with her arms around my waist. I didn't even remember when she'd gotten there. She squeezed me tighter. With her chin resting against my ribs, she said, "You slept through the applause, big guy."

"That you did," said Alex. Her face scrunched around her eyes when she smiled, and for a second I saw her older self in that face. It made my heart hurt.

I held up a hand for a high five. "Congratulations, Miz Kaiser. I knew you could do it."

"We all did," said Galhardo. Fiel chimed in, "You, *Chuugi*, not so much."

"Like hell we didn't," Sage said. She held up the hand Susan wasn't clutching with both of hers. "You should have seen him tough it out when he had to pee."

Everybody broke out into noises then. Some retold the story of the look on my face, and the pounding I had endured. Others laughed at me, and at the telling. Others just laughed. Sensei watched it all, with a joy radiating off of him like heat from a stove. It washed over me, and sent some of the exhaustion and worry away, replacing it with a warm, settled calm.

As the noise began to fade, Sensei stood slightly straighter, and we all got quiet. We could always tell when he was about to speak. He said, "Next time, use the two-in-one trick."

He waited to make sure we were all listening, and when he was, he continued. "You make somebody try to do two things at the same time and he cannot do either correctly. Then you do one thing into that weakness, with all of your will. Only the very best can fight back against this."

We all nodded. I could remember how something like that had made me fail on the mat, or in real life. Then I thought about how time travel does that, making two possibilities in the past impact the future in ways I couldn't control or manage. Heck, even just thinking about time travel did the same thing.

Susan took her chin off my chest and pulled my arm. "I'm taking this one to his bed, in his house, to sleep. We'll see you all tomorrow morning."

Alex said, "I'll pick him up at eight-thirty."

My friends cheered and booed me as she and Alex led me outside. I was asleep again before Alex started her car.

CHAPTER 31

I was dreaming of voices in English, Japanese, Portuguese, and languages I didn't recognize. They were all around me in the dark, talking about I couldn't tell exactly what. Somewhere, the dream shifted into a reality where the voices still spoke, but just in words I knew.

"That's how so many survived," came the voice of Coach Dan Gable. My posters were talking about the war. About the bombing of Nagasaki.

"The bomb missed?" asked Cael Sanderson, legendary collegiate competitor and the first undefeated college wrestler in history.

"By a few hundred yards. Enough for that ridgeline to shield the main population centers," said Coach Gable.

"But so many still died," said Kyle Maynerd, an author and speaker who had wrestled successfully despite having neither arms nor legs.

"Even part of a mountain is only a little bit of a shield against a nuke, son," said Coach.

"How do you know that?" I asked. My voice was rough from sleep and exhaustion.

Cael said, "We're you, buddy. You learned this when you went back in time to hang out at a library."

I want to take a moment and make sure you know my posters don't actually talk to me, and that I don't actually think my posters actually talk to me. There's a lot of weird stuff in my life, like demons and time travel, but my life isn't that weird. I kept posters of these heroes of mine in my room, and somewhere along the line I started talking to them. Before mom and I moved to Portland and I met the Bushido Warriors, they were my best friends and closest advisors.

To the men, I said, "So, you know what's on my mind because you're just in my mind?"

"That would be a yes," Kyle said.

"Does any other interpretation make sense?" said Coach.

"What am I going to do?"

"Well," said Coach, "Here's what's going to happen if you don't do anything."

Cale said, "At elven-oh-two in the morning on August ninth, nineteen-forty-five, a nuclear bomb will explode one thousand, six hundred feet above the city of Nagasaki, Japan. Just over forty thousand people will die that morning, and that number again in the days to follow."

"Among them, your Sensei," said Kyle.

"And probably Alex," Cael said.

"And then, a little more than eighty years later," said Kyle. "You will die, too."

"Unless you do something about it," said Coach.

"Connor, who are you talking to?" I didn't recognize the voice until Alex, my Alex, came into the room. She looked tired, but concerned.

"Uh-oh!" said Kyle. "Busted!"

"Hey, Alex. You're here?"

"Yeah. Susan's asleep on the couch. I realized I was too tired to drive home, so I've been on the easy chair. Your mom picked up a graveyard shift. She says she'll be here for breakfast. That woman is so metal."

I laughed. I'd never thought of Mom being metal, but she really was. She did the hard things, had the hard conversations, solved the hard problems. Even when it wasn't in the family, her job was finding people during the worst days of their lives, and making it better in whatever small or large way she could.

Alex said, "So...who were you talking to?"

"Myself," I said. Even though I knew I wasn't crazy and that my posters weren't really talking. I kept that part of my life to myself.

"Yeah, okay," Alex said. The skepticism was thick in her voice. Then she said, "Can't sleep?"

"Nope."

"I could fix something, if you want. Your mom's tea collection should have what I need." Her eyes fell on the sonic screwdriver, on the floor by my bed and next to my pants. "What you got there? New iPhone?"

"Yeah," I began. I went to get it, then realized I was in my underwear and hesitated just long enough for her to pick it up. As she examined it, her face grew more and more deeply wrinkled with curiosity, then suspicion, then confusion, and then something like awe.

"Hmmmm," she said after what felt like a long time. "Connor, this doesn't exist as far as I know. What gives? The manufacturing stamp on the back is for ninety years from now."

My first thought was to lie, and I let the silence stretch out. But something in the way Alex asked told me I could tell her. Sage and I were much closer as friends, being on the wrestling team together, but Alex had a calmness that made her easy to trust.

Or maybe it was just that a part of me felt like she already sort of knew what was going on, since she would know all about it in the future. "Okay," I said. "But listen until I'm done talking and don't think I'm crazy."

"I can promise one of those," she said. A smile very much like Alex-Sensei's spread across her face.

"Which one?"

"We'll see."

"Okay." I took in a deep breath, then told her all of it. How she showed up in the locker room. How the other *Chuugi* was trying to kill Sensei, but Sensei wouldn't leave. About how I was going to die tomorrow. About how I had lost her in the past, and didn't know how to get back and help her.

Alex's face was grim, but she didn't look like she thought I was crazy. "Well, *Chuugi*," she said when I was done, "what are you going to do about all of that."

"I don't know."

"Me, neither. But we know what we aren't going to do."

"We do?"

"Yes. We're not going to let Sensei die in a storm of nuclear fire."

"I like her," Coach Gable said.

I laughed. I had no idea why I needed to, but I needed to, and I did. Alex smiled while it ran through my face, and my belly, and even my legs. When I finally calmed down, I said, "Okay. Okay. We're not going to do that."

"And we can't let your evil twin conquer the world. Or destroy it...um, was it conquer or destroy?"

"I'm not sure. Maybe both?"

"Well, we can't allow either. And while we're at it, we won't let you die tomorrow."

"No," I said. Alex had a gift for this, a gift I'd seen before. She didn't always come up with the plans. That was usually Fiel or Galhardo. But she could describe the problem, help us organize it in our minds, in a way that made the plans clearer. "I would rather that not happen."

"So you go back, and you find me, and you save the damn day."

"I really like her," Coach Gable said.

"How?" I said. "I can't even unlock this thing."

"One second." She poked the sonic screwdriver, then showed me the open front page.

"What the? How?" I asked.

She shrugged. "It's the same password I use now."

"What is it?"

"None of your business." She poked at the screen for less than a minute, nodded, then showed it to me. "The time travel app — and swear I'm not kidding about that — says the next gate will appear at the convention center in a room in the third sub-basement, late tomorrow morning. I recommend you catch that bus. You'll find it using the map here. And I've disabled the password so you can get in without me, but don't go snooping around in the photos." She handed the sonic screwdriver over.

Coach said, 'I really, really like her."

Alex laughed at the look on my face. "Let me fix you that tea. I'll wake you in time for breakfast."

CHAPTER 32

"Connor! B minus two minutes!" Mom's voice slid into my deep and dreamless sleep. I woke up feeling surprisingly good. My muscles and joints still felt tired, but the pain and the utter exhaustion were gone. From the bathroom, I heard what sounded like dozens of voices out at the breakfast table. Finished, I went out and found it was just five.

Mom and Susan were chatting at the table, eating plates full of eggs and sausage. Mrs. D. was in the kitchen scooping more onto a plate. She reached them toward me just as Alex and Avo stopped in the middle of a conversation and beckoned me toward an empty chair. Alex rolled up the sleeve of my pants leg while Avo cracked open a jar full of pungent herbs. They both made identical clucking noises while the older woman poked my joints and muscles.

Alex said to Avo, *"Inchado mais do que esperavamos."*

Susan had been in the kitchen with Mrs. D. She brought out a big stack of French toast with berries and slid in between me and Alex. The smell made my stomach cramp with hunger. It had been more hours than I could count since I had eaten real food.

Avo said to Alex, *"Mas menos do que temiamos."*

I kept my leg out and ate huge forkfuls of carbohydrates. I could feel it feeding my body with every bite, while Alex and Avo kept working on my leg. They did better without my opinions, which they always ignored anyway.

Alex said, *"Isso deve fazer por agora, mas vai doe amanha."*

Avo said to Alex, *"Mas nao vamos contar a ele sobre a amanha. Ele esta bem por hoje."*

"How's he doing?" Mom asked. She scooped up my empty plate and replaced it with one full of sausage and scrambled eggs.

"It'll hold for today," Alex said to Mom. All three women were talking like I wasn't even in the room. "But we should both try to not let him do much for the next few weeks."

Avo clucked and shook a finger at Alex, saying, *"Exceto por seus exercicios."*

"Yes, Avo," Alex said to her, "Except for his exercises."

Mom said, "I don't understand it, but it's good enough for me. Thank you both. Avo, *obrigado*."

Avo smiled around her nearly toothless mouth. Alex nodded her head once. I just sat there, feeling a weird combination of love and fear. I was being fed, cared for, and celebrated by some of the people closest to me, but at the same time what happened between now and the end threatened them all, and was completely on me. I could not fail them.

Susan put one hand high up on the thigh of my good leg. "You good to go, champ?" She gave me a look that said she wasn't just talking about wrestling.

Mom gave me one of her mom looks, holding my eyes with hers while she seemed to stare all the way past my pupils and into my thoughts. "Are you ready for this, kiddo? You were absolutely wiped out last night. You look nervous."

Of course I looked nervous. I was going to die later that day. I tried to smile the look off my face, but Mom squinted at me while Avo gave me a wrinkly side-eye. They weren't buying it.

Avo said, "You fight the fight good, yes?"

Mrs. D. nudged Susan out of her chair and sat down, a cooked sausage wobbling in one hand. She waved it at me and said, "How do you say it, strange boy? You have it?"

"Do you mean he's got this?" Alex said. Susan smiled and took her hand off my shoulder to stifle a giggle.

"Just so," Mrs. D. said. "Strange boy, my Connor. You got this." She bit off half the sausage in one bite and chewed it. She and Avo shared a glance together while she chewed, something passing between them that felt like Sensei. I remembered how Mrs. D. had fought a demon for me, and the magic Avo used on my leg. These were women of power, like Mom. Like Alex-Sensei.

In that moment I felt a part of my shoulders relax like they hadn't in days. Something in my stomach settled that I hadn't realized had been upset. Everybody in this room was on my side. Even if I failed today. Even if I died, a part of things would be okay because they would make it okay. My next bite of eggs and sausage tasted better, and my stomach accepted it more fully. I relaxed into the feeling, and another layer of tiredness faded away.

In the car ride to the tournament with Susan and Alex, I almost felt like I was going to pull this off. The presence of my friends, and the love and respect they had for me, built me up. Nobody had to say anything in particular. Just their voices made me stronger, made me bigger, healed me.

Mom did that to me, too. It was the opposite of my dad, who could make me feel tiny and afraid just by being near me, even though I'd been bigger than him since my fifteenth birthday.

As I walked into the tournament, I saw the dozens of athletes cutting the air with their motion, heard the buzz and cheer of the audience. I could smell sweat and anticipation, feel the excitement in the air. More than all the stuff I can describe using my senses, there was an optimism in this place. All the wrestlers were feeling a sense of potential, of what could happen that day, and it filled the open space with something like the opposite of fear. I stood in the entry for a few long breaths, taking it in. If *oni* could feed on the bad things in life, maybe I could feed on those good things. Maybe it could help give me the energy, the power to do what I would have to do today.

Coach found me and put his hand on my shoulders, squeezing them in that half-massage way people sometimes do. "Did you get enough rest?"

I felt my shoulders release under the pressure. I felt so good after the food and Alex's tea. "Born ready, coach. I'm at one hundred percent."

"Good. You're up soon."

"Calling Connor Morgan and Ezekiel Phan," said a voice on the PA.

"See?" Coach told me. "Coach is always right."

CHAPTER 33

I walked to my match, feeling the cheers from the bleachers fill the space with positive energy. I looked up to find Susan, paired with Alex, Fiel, and Galhardo. I waved to them just as Sage came up and high-fived the same hand.

The mat was right there, with Phan already on the line at its center. He was from Crater Lake, a big school we didn't wrestle against during the regular season. He had a reputation as being good, but not quite as good as me. I wondered for a few seconds if any of it mattered. In the face of the battle between good and evil, in the face of Sensei's possible death, my death, Mom's heartbreak if I didn't live, what did it matter if I won or lost a wrestling match?

I strapped on my headgear and stepped forward, because it mattered to me.

Mattering to me and mattering, really mattering, weren't the same thing. Not the same thing at all. But I thought of the men in that POW camp from last night...um, from 70 years ago. They had to have wondered if waking up another day really mattered, if taking the easier way out wouldn't have been better. But they didn't. Sometimes things matter most when they don't seem to matter at all. What you do then is how you stand up in your own eyes for the rest of your life.

My grandmother used to tell me a story about my grandfather, about how he had come to America with so little, worked so hard to give Mom, and then me, a better life. How sometimes she used to say that working one more day wouldn't matter, and how he would tell her it mattered so much because it mattered so little.

Mom took that heritage, even though it was only hers from a marriage she was running away from. She made sure I knew it was important, even with the trouble and pain my father had caused her. She did so many things, worried about so much, made the little pieces matter so we were ready when the big things came up. Big things like my dad going to prison, our apartment. A scholarship for me would make her job so much easier.

So I was going to wrestle my best. Because the little things matter.

I reached the line and put out my hand. Phan shook it. From the side, Coach shouted, "He's a thrower, Connor! Take him down early and fight your fight."

The whistle blew and I shot low and hard for Phan's ankles. He was quick, shooting his legs back and pushing off of me. He grabbed my wrist as we stood back up and didn't let go for the rest of the first round. We circled and probed, but nothing else happened until the action broke at 0-0.

Phan won the toss for round two, and chose down position. We set up, him on his hands and knees and me behind and above him with one hand around his waist and one on his elbow. He shot up hard and fast on the whistle, breaking free of my grip before I'd even realized the round had started. On his feet, he grabbed my wrist again and held on to me, not letting me move. The referee warned him for stalling, but the round ended with Phan in the lead, 0-1.

I chose both up for the final round, hoping for a two-point takedown to win the match, but he grabbed my wrist again and started the same dance we've been moving to for almost 4 minutes already. He held on, pulling me slightly forward and stopping me from shooting for a takedown or closing for a throw. All he had to do was keep holding me for another 100 seconds and he would win.

Coach and Sage shouted at me with a frenzied mixture of advice and pure frustration, but I couldn't make out the exact words. I tried to wrench my wrist free but his two hands were stronger than my one. Phan's coach shouted, "One minute left! Keep it up!"

I was running out of time. I remembered what Sensei had said about making people think of two things at once, how it made them do neither well. It was worth trying. Nothing else I'd done so far had worked.

We circled twice as I figured out how to try the technique. Outside, from what felt like far away, Coach yelled, "Thirty seconds Morgan! Make it happen!"

I pushed on Phan's face with my free hand, cupped the back of his head and yanked down hard. As he rose to resist, I tightened my grip on his grabbing hands and shot low, thrusting my free arm between his legs in a fireman's carry. I hoisted him over my shoulders and dropped him to the mat for two points. He scrambled to his belly before I could go for the pin and the whistle blew at 2-1. I shook his hand, and the ref raised mine.

The raised hand felt as good as it always did. Even in the middle of a battle through time with my friends, Mom, and the world at stake, that small affirmation sent a surge of happiness through me. If I'd been *looking*, I might have seen hundreds of *oni* fleeing that joy like the blast radius of the world's least harmful bomb.

Alex was with Sage as I came off the mat, pointing to her wrist even though she doesn't wear a watch. She peeled me away as soon as we could without raising suspicion from our friend. As we entered the service hallway, she handed me the sonic screwdriver.

"I took the liberty of fiddling with this while you were asleep. Here's what I know. It works just like a cell phone. The password is 192837. The app with the hourglass icon, and I'm not kidding about that, looks automatically set up to guide you."

"Okay."

As we passed a uniformed woman pushing a cart of supplies, I grabbed a box of big pretzel salts with one hand. Mrs. D. had used salt to save me the day I found out she was probably a witch, and I used some to save myself later on. It wasn't the world's most intimidating weapon, but seems to work just fine against demons. My stomach tightened as I wondered how it worked against fallen Bushido Champions.

Alex led me through a pair of metal doors seeming to know exactly where we needed to go. I had never gone wrong with trusting her in the past. Not with my recovery. Not with having my back in a fight. Heck, not even with the answers to a chemistry final.

"It's pretty intuitive to use, Connor, but you won't really need it because you're going to find me — Sensei future me — and we'll use it to get us both home after you save the world."

We turned the corner into a dead end storage space. The gate was already there, about the size of Alex's head and glowing faintly. She said to me, "Are you sure I shouldn't come with you?"

"You seemed pretty serious about that being a no."

Alex smiled. "And I'm pretty smart. I'll have to trust me. I already checked when and where you'll be coming back, and I won't be there. Let me know how it turns out, okay?"

From what she had told me, from what the other she had told me, neither of us would remember anything. I wouldn't know what to tell, and she wouldn't know she was supposed to ask. But I nodded and hugged my friend as the room glowed brighter in the light of the glowing gate.

"Okay," I said.

"Okay," I said to Alex. We turned it together to look at the gate, now full-sized. A dark space with the suggestion of a wall showed in its tiny center.

"Connor?" Alex said.

"Yes, Alex?" I squeezed my friend's hand. It was time to go save her life. And Sensei's. And mine.

"Does it hurt to go through?"

I smiled. "Only a little."

CHAPTER 34

Jumping only hurt a little that time, just like I told Alex. At least it only hurt a little in comparison to the tackle that hit me the instant my feet hit the ground in the past. Something huge, and made of sharp armor plates, slammed into my chest and drove me to the ground. Before I could even take a breath, it was rolling around on me and cutting through my clothes. It sliced shallow cuts into my skin even as I struggled to recover from the jump.

I rolled to my stomach so my attacker would hit the big muscles and bones in my back instead of my more vulnerable parts, then pushed up to my hands and knees. The demon clung to my back and dug short claws into my shoulders and butt. Around me, the shadows of other *oni* crowded close. One swept my arm out from under me and they piled on as I fell to my face in the dirt.

I turned the fall into a shoulder roll, flinging monsters off me as I rolled again and got to my feet. I was surrounded by dozens, maybe a hundred *oni* of every shape and size you can imagine, and many you wouldn't ever want to. My box of salt was on the ground where I landed, maybe three steps and ten demons away.

Sometimes the only way out is through. I shouted a sharp kiai, a "spirit shout" like you see in the old karate movies. When you do one wrong, you feel like an idiot. When you do it right, all of your courage, and your focus, and your determination come out of you in what feels like a solid wall of sound. It makes you stronger, literally stronger, in your mind and body. And it scares the fight right out of cowardly opponents like *oni*.

It froze enough of them just long enough for me to dive through and grab the box of salt, but three were already hanging from my head and neck by the time I tore it open. I rose to my feet, spinning in a fast circle with the box top open. White crystals sprayed out in a spiraling line, splashing the demons all around me.

Nasty black smoke and thin screams filled the air. About half of the demons died right then, dissipating into greasy smears, while the others ran squealing into the night. The *oni* on me leapt for the nearest rooftop, but I managed to spear one with a high kick as it went.

Alone but for a few trembling demons trying to become invisible in the shadows, I jogged into the nearest alley.

As I ran, I checked the sonic screwdriver. Alex had been right. The hourglass icon worked about the same way as the maps app on my phone, although I couldn't even guess how it got signal in 1945. I followed its directions through the night, running when the streets were clear and slowing to a creep when I heard footsteps. I moved faster than I thought I would, my mind drifting as I went to think about the sleeping people in the houses so close to me.

Those people, those families, were probably relieved they weren't in the war and in immediate danger. They'd been bombed, the city was full of the signs, but none would have to fight. How would they feel in the morning, those who could feel anything at all?

I ran out of the city, the sonic screwdriver leading me on the same path Alex and I had taken the night before...which was the same night as now...but almost a day later and still years earlier.

I had to stop thinking about things that way.

No sound came from the jungle, not even the sounds of night animals rustling in the underbrush. Even my footsteps felt unnaturally muffled by the leaves on the path. Nothing attacked me, or moved in the shadows as I made my way steadily to the cave, feeling the fatigue from all my efforts settle into the muscles of my butt, and legs, and back.

When I reached the clearing by the cave, I waited at the tree line. Nothing moved. The night stayed too quiet to be real. I waited for a count of one hundred breaths, then crept up to the cave mouth and poked my head inside.

The piles of rocks were still there, undisturbed except for a pool of toppled stones beneath where the gate had been when I drove through. What wasn't there, was Alex.

"Alex?" I called. She could have been hiding, but would have seen me and come out when I entered the cave. She wasn't there, and she didn't come. Faint sounds echoed from the camp below, the only noises in the night other than my breath, but no sign of my friend.

I tapped the screen of the Sonic Screwdriver, hoping to bring up a map I could use to start searching for Alex. Maybe she had entered checkpoints, or even directions. Maybe she'd left a note reminding me to bring snacks she missed. The light from the screen showed me the answer: a message from the future, written here in the past.

The cave wall was covered in black lines of soot from fires people had lit. In one black patch somebody had scrubbed off lines to make a word.

Lo23R DoJo

It was English. Well, sort of English. Leetspeak. In a cave in Japan in 1945. It could only be from Alex. "Loser" would mean me. "Dojo" was where I could find her.

"Okay," I said aloud. I knew where my friend was.

"Okay," Said another voice as a shadow blocked the moonlight at the mouth of the cave.

I smiled and turned, expecting to find Alex. But it wasn't Alex. It was *Chuugi*, but a *Chuugi* who had changed since I last saw him storming out of the dojo.

He stood now a head taller than me, and seemed twice as wide in his battle gear. His black lacquer armor and helmet gleamed, but not just from the moonlight. It glowed but didn't glow, casting shadows while somehow shedding no real light. His face was invisible except for eyes that glowed with the same red light as our lantern the moment before it shattered. Twin swords hung from his belt, one long and curved and the other a smaller twin: the katana and wakizashi of a samurai.

"Chuugi," he said, his voice simultaneously a whisper and a powerful shout. "Here, together and alone, we are the same."

CHAPTER 35

"But that is a lie," The giant warrior said. "I am no more *Chuugi* than the infant your mother birthed as the man standing before me now. *Chuugi* was weak. Indecisive. Full of self-doubt."

I leapt at him. This was no time to talk. I faked high like I was punching for his throat, then drove as low as I could to grab his ankle. In a wrestling match, that would let me take him down for points. In that cave on that night I could use things I had learned from Sensei and Galhardo to break his ankle and dislocate his hip. It wouldn't kill him, but it would stop him from chasing me while I ran back down the mountain toward Alex and Sensei.

Only I never even got his ankle. He leaned down almost casually and plucked my wrist out of the air. Using all the power, speed, and momentum I had put into the dive, he flipped me backwards and slammed me to the ground of the cave. Piles of stone scattered everywhere, rattling off the walls with the same sound my bones were making inside my body. He stood above me, not doing anything, but radiating the possibility of what he could do if he wanted.

I lay there and waited for my lungs to find breath again.

"You must be from another time," he said. "I can feel you in me. Can you feel it, too? Or are you still too weak and untrained to experience the real world?"

I could feel it. I did not like it. His English was perfect, or maybe he was speaking in Japanese and I understood him perfectly behind and beneath the sounds of the words, from a connection running between us like a string between two tin cans. His meaning, his anger, his power, they all reached out to me and vibrated inside my being, my *tan dien*. It made me queasy while at the same time replacing the fatigue and pain in my body with a righteous anger. It warmed me, and pushed gentle feelings out of my mind, filling me instead with a hot, flowing power. I felt what he might want me to feel, what Fiel and Galhardo probably would have called the Dark Side for reasons they never explained to me.

"Two *Chuugis* in one time," he said as he looked down at me. Despite the mask over his face, I could feel the curiosity passing over him, could sense the gears of his mind working to fit me into his plans. "It must be *unmei*."

The last time a Demon Lord had monologued at me, I'd punched it in its yapping face. This time, I was still struggling to recover my breath from the body slam, and to somehow make my mind work in the face of this weird connection.

"Why else would the fates align to put you here with me, to see the being you might become, if not for you to join me in the changing of the world for the better?"

"Fate probably wants me to kick your ass," I wheezed. It wasn't the smartest thing I've ever said, but it was honest.

"You...you joke," he stuttered. "But you must see the truth of it. The kamikazes were my idea. Their loyalty is a beautiful thing, but not for such as I. And it should not be for you, unless you insist on making it so."

My breath strengthened even as he talked, and I felt control of my muscles return. There was a narrow gap to his left. If I could roll through it—

He shifted just inches, enough to block that line of escape. "Not so fast, little me. You've spent your life looking for those strong enough to earn and hold your trust, who can keep you safe from the darknesses of the world. Trust in fate. Trust in me. Who would know better what you need than yourself?"

A part of me believed him in that moment. Trust had helped me leave with Mom when the time to escape from my dad finally came. Trust was how my wrestling improved when I listened to what my coaches told me. It was trust that had allowed me to join the Bushido Warriors when they first told me I was part of an ancient war against demons. Wasn't trusting people exactly what made me *Chuugi*? Wasn't it?

"Yes," said the other *Chuugi*. "Exactly. I see your mind. Loyalty is trust. Trust in your betters."

Maybe if I trusted my other self in that moment, he would help me save Sensei.

"Trust in yourself, in becoming part of something larger. Be the strongest link in a chain that has held power for thousands of years."

He had a point. I'd traded up joining the Bushido Champions. Mom had traded us both up when we'd abandoned my dad. Was he just offering me a chance to trade up again?

"Trust in power, in discovering what you can become if only I give you the will to take it."

I shook my head, hard, trying to clear it. He was making too much sense. If I had enough power, I could help Mom in so many ways. I could even help the Bushido Warriors, no matter what this monster wanted.

"Loyalty is power, *Chuugi*. I am power. We, together, in this time or in yours, could become more powerful than even the greatest demons of the outer dark. Be loyal to yourself, and loyal to me. We could rule Nippon, and ultimately the world if you can find the strength to turn your back on these weaklings."

I'm not a smart person, but I know what's right. I had seen smart people twist words and ideas until what was wrong felt right, and I recognized it even in that dark place, coming from somebody who was essentially myself.

"Now," the other *Chuugi* said, "Decipher for me the code your master left for you. I will admit, it is ingenious. The Bushido Champions are not unformidable."

I had to laugh. He had shown his weakness.

"Tell me and I will show you power you have never imagined existed. Refuse me one moment longer and your suffering will be like unto—"

I kipped up to my feet and leapt towards the cave mouth. I knew I'd be too slow to make it through, but if I made it far enough I could use his reaction. He caught me by the leg and shoulder, flipping me in midair. He used my momentum to throw me, but my plan had worked, forcing him to sling my body past him and into the clearing outside. I hit the ground rolling, rode the force up to my feet, and ran like...well, um, like a fallen Bushido Champion bent on my personal destruction was right on my tail.

CHAPTER 36

I ran hard down the jungle path toward Nagasaki and the dojo, Alex, and Sensei. The other *Chuugi* was far more powerful than me, faster, meaner, and right on my heels. But if I could reach the dojo, with Alex's help and maybe even Sensei's if he realized what his *Chuugi* had become, the giant warrior couldn't possibly be a match for all three of us.

Could he?

My back burned in the lines of my symbol, hotter than it had in the cave. A power that swept through me in waves of ice and fire, over and over again. *Chuugi* had to be farther away from me than he had been in the cave, but maybe his attention or anger has changed things. It felt like being branded, the pain making me stumble even though my path was clear. I caught myself on a tree, hearing him crash on the trail behind me, then sprinted full out. Maybe his attention or anger has changed things.

When I reached the switchback trail, I took it in a series of long leaps and slides, barely holding my balance. One slip, and I'd be in a short misery, lying broken at the bottom before my evil twin put me out of it. I forced myself to focus on not slipping instead of what would happen if I did, placing each foot carefully as I half-ran, half-tumbled down the slope.

I was halfway down when a thundering *kiai* shook the air. I felt more than saw *Chuugi* leap through the air above me. He landed in a crouch at the bottom of the trail, taking a powerful stance to block my way.

Still two turns from the bottom, I realized I would have to get past him. And he would have all the time in the world to be ready for me to try.

As I ran the straightaway, I scooped up a rock and threw it at his face. He slipped his head with a contemptuous snort and dodged. At the turn, I threw another. He shuffled sideways a fraction of an inch. The stones sailed harmlessly past his ear and into the trees behind.

At the final turn, I threw a third rock, this time aiming for his chest. He dodged with his head, and it hit him square in the center of his black, lacquered armor.

It couldn't have hurt him, and probably wouldn't have hurt him if he had been naked, but he howled in annoyance at having been tricked. It was just enough distraction that when I tucked into a shoulder roll I made it past him. He grabbed at me but missed by inches, or maybe 3 miles. It didn't matter. I was past him and running faster than I had ever run before.

I reached the stone streets of the city and picked up my pace now that my footing was clear. Behind me I imagined I could hear paving stones breaking under his heavy boots. He felt further away though, like I was a little bit faster on the paved ground.

As we ran, I kept passing people out in the city at night. They were all walking in the same direction I was running, and there were far more than I had ever seen before in the city at night. I was afraid *Chuugi* had cast some kind of spell to move them against Sensei, against me, but nobody attacked as I ran. They noticed me, many shouting in surprise as a huge person who was clearly not Japanese appeared out of the night, but none tried to stop me.

The park was crowded with men, women, and children, all looking toward the dojo and walking in that direction. I pushed through them as gently as I could, parting the smaller, hungry people like waves in front of a tugboat. So many were surrounding the dojo, soldiers and civilians in a growing crowd. They were awake and out in the blacked-out city. I didn't know what was happening, but as I reached the edge of the trees I expected another fight.

But then I saw them, really saw the people around me. I didn't have to *look*. I just had to see the moment with my full attention. What I saw wasn't a mob surrounding the dojo ready to attack. It was a frightened crowd carrying bags, boxes, and crates. A few people stood at the top of the dojo stairs, between *Um* and *Ah*, receiving the packages from those below. Others near them sorted the gifts into piles on the street. These people were there to help. With what, I didn't know, but I intended to find out.

As I reached the bottom of the stairs, Alex came out carrying a huge wooden chest as if it were weightless. She handed it down to three men, who struggled to set it on the ground. When she stood up, she saw me.

"You got my message." A smile split her face, just like it did when her younger self saw something beautiful she couldn't help but tell us about.

I doubled over, gasping and trying to speak, pointing toward the park behind me. Alex's brow wrinkled as she tried to understand, but then it all became obvious.

Chuugi broke through the tree line, running hard and seeming as large and unstoppable as a bullet train. The men and women all around turned away from him as if burned by the terrible power he radiated in waves. They shuffled out of his way and left an open lane between him and the dojo stairs. I forced myself to stand up in a fighting stance. My legs shook from exhaustion, but my nerves were steady. I was with my friend, about to fight the good fight, ready for...well, for whatever came next.

Behind and above me the door opened, and I could feel Sensei there without having to turn and look.

Chuugi slowed to a swaggering walk, huge as he moved between the huddled civilians to either side. He waved his hands and the people scattered further back.

Next to me, Ah and Um's eyes and mouths flared with orange fire.

Power swept over me, the same hot, taut low as I had felt in the cave. It didn't even move a hair on my arms, but pushed away my confidence and strength, my decision to fight. My legs sagged and my heart sank, but another wave of power hit me from the other direction. This one was its opposite, filling me with love and hope. Then the first wave crashed over me again. I was less surprised this time, better able to deal with the hopelessness and despair. My legs stayed strong, but I wasn't sure I could use them, make them move under the crushing weight of this emotional assault.

I tried anyway. Every inch was like moving through mud up to my neck but I put one foot in front of the other. *Chuugi's* eyes widened in surprise, then narrowed with anger as even more hot energy hit me like a wall. I couldn't move even a toe, and then the warmth of Sense's power passed through me and over me.

"*Chuugi*!", Sensei shouted, and somehow I knew he was talking to the dark warrior in front of us. "You have the power to stop this!"

Our foe said nothing, instead of taking advantage of the focus Sensei's words took from the fight to push the wave of energy forward. It ripped through me with a feeling like a muscle cramp, only in the middle of my soul. Then Sensei and Alex pushed back together, and the pain stopped. It was such a relief I nearly fell over. Then *Chuugi* pushed even harder, and the pain slammed through me again.

Back and forth. Pain and relief. Light and Darkness. They passed back and forth over me so many times I lost count. It was all I could do just stay upright as my nerves jerked like marionette strings somebody kept setting on fire. I didn't know how much more I could take before either my mind or my body just quit on me.

Then beneath it all, *Chuugi's* voice whispered silently in my mind. "This can stop. You can stop it. Your friends can't even help you now, here together in their place of power." The spiritual cramp intensified, wracking my mind. I wanted to scream, but couldn't figure out how to make my body do it.

Then I heard a noise, a real sound, coming from behind me. It sounded like Alex screaming but that wasn't quite right.

She was *singing*.

"I won't do what you tell me!" something like healing fire walked over me, then receded. *Chuugi's* power hit me again, a wall of pain.

"*Chuugi!*" Alex shouted to me. "You know the words!"

The confusion warred with my pain long enough for me to gasp, "Is...that...the...Dead...Kennedys?"

She sighed in disappointment even as her fiery energy lapped at my back and, together, we screamed the climax into the air in a way that felt so familiar, so much like spending time with my friends after practice at the dojo, I had to laugh. The pain didn't vanish, but it lessened. Of course I had the band's name wrong, but Alex was right about me knowing the lyrics. She and I shouted and sang together, a song the world around us wouldn't hear for more than fifty years.

"Fuck you! I won't do what you tell me!" We sang in unison, the power of the words and our friendship and our love for each other rolling together into a force

Chuugi could do nothing about. Where it clashed with the fallen warrior's energy, it glowed bright pink in a visible arc. It pushed down the stairs, through me, and into his chest. *Chuugi* faltered, took two staggering backwards steps, and fell to one knee.

My body sagged, the power of the conflict no longer holding me upright while my muscles stayed slack from the exhaustion and pain. I caught myself before I fell, and stood up straight. I glanced behind me. Sensei and Alex-Sensei stood ready, solid but relaxed in fighting stances.

Then *Chuugi* stood, drawing both swords with a roar I could almost see. He leapt to the attack as waves of force shot forward with a sweep of his blades. Sensei was slammed into and through the dojo door. Alex fell off the stairs.

It was up to me.

Chuugi charged us, literally alight with power and fury. He seemed even bigger than he had been, bigger than the trees behind him, and moved with such speed and anger it was like looking at a hurricane from way too close up.

I dug my heels into the cobblestones, breathed deep, and stood between this monster and my mentors.

CHAPTER 37

I crouched, preparing myself for impact as *Chuugi* charged in. Between us, his swords wove a pattern of a flashing danger. I know it's impossible, but I swear I could feel his breath even from that distance. It was hot, steaming, and somehow simultaneously furious and filled with pain. I felt fear like I hadn't since my dad used to hit Mom when I was too small to stop him. It clawed through my stomach, filling my throat and choking off my breath like I was vomiting terror. It threatened to take me over completely.

Chuugi's footsteps rang like thunder. He swung his two wicked swords in a smooth, unified motion. One tip flicked a stone from the ground which I barely dodged with a slip of my head even as my legs shook beneath me.

From behind me came the sound of a stone hitting flesh, followed by Alex's voice in a scream. Anger joined the fear and they ran through me. My stomach shaking and my eyes watering, I breathed them both out so they passed through me and over me instead of sticking into my mind and spirit, weighing me down.

Chuugi planted one foot hard enough to shatter the stone beneath it, then leapt into the air with both swords raised for a killing blow.

I screamed myself into action and I jumped forward to where *Chuugi's* thighs met his hips. It was an easier move to defend against then the ankle pick he had countered so easily earlier, but he had both his hands full and was literally in midair. I caught him hard right where I wanted to and all of my weight and strength worked with his inertia to fold him in half. We crashed to the ground with an impact that shook the buildings and my bones. His swords skidded out of his hands and I scrambled to get on top of him, but he rolled and sent me tumbling across the cobblestones to slam into the base of the dojo stairs.

I jumped up immediately and ran at him again. As I closed the distance, a wave of magical pressure blew past me from behind. At least one of my Senseis was back in the fight. *Chuugi* took two side steps back, fighting the assault. When I reached him, he backhanded me hard enough I missed to his right, but the move stole his focus and he slid back several feet.

Both Alex and Sensei stood together at the top of the stairs, throwing everything they had against the aura of our enemy. Something in *Chuugi*'s stance told me he was preparing a counterstrike even under their combined force. If he had power to muster under their combined strength, I could not let him actually throw that punch.

I shot to the left, then spun right and took two steps forward. As he swung at my head, I dropped into a roll beneath his arms. It took me behind him and over one of his swords, which I picked up as I passed. I stood up, surprised it had worked so well, and just in time for *Chuugi* to grab my wrist. He swung my arm in a circle that sent the sword flying toward Alex. It hit her, hilt first, but hard enough to knock her to the ground. I fell and rolled again, feeling my shoulder wrench as I pulled it from *Chuugi*'s iron grasp.

The energy around me shifted, with Alex down and Sensei distracted by her pain. *Chuugi* gave me his full and undivided attention, lashing out with a kick that felt like...well...um, something that kicks harder than anything I'd ever been kicked by.

I stumbled backward, riding some of the impact and landing in a tight roll. I got to my feet just in time to dodge a second kick, then a vicious elbow that might have taken my head off if I had kept it in one place an instant longer. I gasped, "Help me!" to Alex, but she didn't respond.

If she was conscious, her entire focus was on keeping herself in the fight. I heard Sensei's voice somehow in my mind and not in my ears as I ducked under another elbow strike and slipped sideways to avoid the palm heel that had been the real attack. "It can't be me, *Chuugi*. It must be you."

When he said our name, a burst of energy passed between me and *Chuugi*. He faltered for a split-second, but the same vibration filled me with warmth and drove the pain out of my body. I shuffled forward until my chest was almost touching his belly, and grabbed both of his wrists. I held on tight and leapt backward while throwing my heels into his hips and landing on my back. The sacrifice throw surprised the giant warrior, and I pulled him over me, hoping to toss him into the Senseis. I still didn't know how, but I ended up being the one who got thrown. I went through the air and hit the ground with such an impact I didn't just see stars. I heard and smelled them too. But I couldn't stay still, not for a moment. I rolled sideways just as one of *Chuugi*'s feet crashed down like an avalanche, then I reversed direction and grabbed his ankle with both arms.

This time I got him. I stood as tall as I could, picking up *Chuugi*'s leg until it was at the height of his shoulders. I pushed it up further and aimed to kick his other knee as hard as I could. He turned just slightly and I missed. I lost my balance and we both fell down again. As we landed, *Chuugi* punctuated the impact with a spirit yell so loud and powerful it rang the bell of the temple next door.

Alex screamed in pain, the first sound that told me she was even still alive. I glanced back to see Sensei down on one knee, shaking his head.

I pushed to my feet. *Chuugi* was still on the ground beside me, but something was wrong. He smiled with anger, hate, and an absolute certainty that I was his now that both Senseis were out of the fight.

I took a fighting position, not hoping for much but to let Sensei and *Chuugi* know that I chose to fight him to the last.

He began to sit up. Just as I raised my fists to get ready, a stone paw slammed down on the center of his chest, pressing him back to the ground. Despite the straining cords of his muscles, it held him in place.

"*Nandeshoo?!?*" he shouted, struggling against the weight. I didn't know the exact words, but his wide eyes and snarling face showed the confusion, rage, and a little bit of fear.

The paw was the size of my head, and made of pitted, scarred granite. My eyes followed up its leg to a stony, shaggy chest, thick neck, and mane of curly hair. It was *Um*. Or maybe *Ah*. No. *Um* had a chip on his foot this one didn't. *Ah* snarled, baring sharp teeth beneath eyes glowing red with ferocious power.

Ah had *Chuugi* dead to rights. Mighty as he was, huge and strong, he could only snarl and squirm under the multi-ton weight of the ancient stone guardian.

A hand weighed gently on my shoulder. It was Sensei, standing beside me and looking down. Tears streaked his wrinkled face.

"Stop this, *Chuugi*," he said to the warrior. "Come home. There is so much yet to do. "

Chuugi just laughed, a ringing, sick sound that made *Ah* cock his stony grey head in what might have been confusion.

Sensei's face grew stern. He inhaled deeply and clapped his hand as he shouted, "*Kare o Tebanasu!*"

"*Ika sete!*" *Chuugi* said, in a tone that somehow exactly matched sensei's but mocked him at the same time. His face twisted with concentration for a moment, then he disappeared in a puff of smoke. It was like when I killed demons, but the smoke moved like it was alive, slithering against the wind and out of sight.

I looked to Sensei, but he shook his head. "He will be hours returning to physical form. We are safe, for now."

I fell to my knees and leaned my head against *Ah*. It was inert again, unmoving stone. I reached up one hand and scratched it under the chin.

"Who's a good boy, then?" I said.

"Girl," Alex rasped from where she lay nearby.

CHAPTER 38

Alex got up first, smoothly and silently though she must have hurt at least as much as I did. She walked toward me, slowly at first, but gaining strength and confidence with each step. She held up a fist for me to bump.

I forced myself to my feet, and gave her my hand. When our knuckles came apart, I jerked my head toward *Ah*, still in the middle of the street.

"Did he just?" I said.

"Yes," Alex answered. The mysterious smile on her face was exactly like Sensei's.

"No, really. I know I saw it but did I really just see the —"

"Yes," she said again.

Sensei slipped lightly past us and opened the dojo door. Behind us, the road began to fill once again with people. "Come in," he said. "Come in, both of you."

I stumbled, my bad leg twinging like something had just bitten it. Despite being less than half my size, Alex slid in to support me like I weighed nothing. Together, we walked into the dojo.

Like I had noticed just hours before with the dojo at home, the distance in time and space meant nothing. The dark beams and straw mats, the punching bags and training dummies, the low tea table, all greeted me like old friends I'd been away from for too long.

The only real difference was the supplies. Where before there had been empty space, here it was filled. Crates full of limp, small vegetables filled the sumo ring. On the training floor, canvas sacks full of bandages, cloth, rope, and tools stood in neat rows. Canned goods and ceramic pots formed orderly ranks in front of the door to Sensei's room.

Alex slid in between Sensei and the tea cabinet. "Sensei, I will serve. "

Sensei paused, looking as surprised as I had ever seen him, but he studied her face and simply said, "You know how?"

"You taught me."

Sensei nodded, slowly, and gestured to the tea cabinet with one wizened hand. Then he pointed to me, and the piles of supplies. Even with the slight differences from the dojo in my time, even filled with crates and bags and boxes, this was my home. It was my home in 1945, more than half a century before I would even be born.

Because of my dad, Mom had moved the two of us around so much I've never really had a physical home. Mom was my home. My room, with my posters, was my home. The wrestling team was my home. Only after joining the Bushido Warriors had I found a physical space that felt that way, and here I had found it again in the past.

"Where did all this come from?" I asked, as I surveyed the assembled supplies.

"The people," Sensei said. He took a seat at the low table, along the side where Sage and Galhardo usually sat.

I took my place across from him, leaving the head for Alex, who joined us a moment later. She poured the tea and passed cups to each of us. I asked, "They kept it aside?"

After a first long sip, Sensei said, "Yes."

I thought about what a huge burden that must have been. Keeping food in the house when you're hungry, when the people around you are starving, when you could be punished or killed if the authorities found out you were hoarding valuable goods. The temptation and the risk must have been a constant struggle.

I asked, "And now they're giving it to you? Just giving it?"

"Not to me. To those I may need to give it to tomorrow."

"But how?" was all I could say.

Sensei spoke to both of us, but it felt like his words were meant for me alone. "A warrior doesn't only fight. A warrior leads. People know they can trust his judgment because he weighs life and death every day. They will do as a warrior says. More importantly, they will do as he does."

I drank my tea, feeling the warmth from the fluid seep through my stomach and into my tired, aching limbs. A little bit of life returned to them. I thought about that while I finished my cup. Just as I swallowed the last mouthful, there was a knock at the door.

Sensei stood to open it for a group of boys in ragged clothing. He spoke to them in Japanese and gestured to the piled supplies. The boys started moving them outside, fire brigade style, and Sensei returned to his place at the table.

"I know why you are here," he said to us. His face was grave.

"Yes," I said. "We need to tell you about *Chuugi* — about the other *Chuugi*. How he..."

"How he has fallen," Sensei said. The sorrow on his face was deep as the ocean.

"Yes," I said.

Sensei breathed deeply in and sighed. "And you have come to say I should leave before tomorrow's catastrophe, that I am staying under the advice of a traitor?"

"Um....yes, Sensei." I stammered.

"You will fail in this intention, *Chuugi*," he said firmly, but gently and without anger. "I am needed here. These supplies, these people. My help. All will be needed in the days to come, if what you tell me will happen comes to pass." He was right, but something nagged at the back of my brain. Something that said he could do both if I could only remember something important I was forgetting.

Alex put her teacup down in a way that slammed it against the table without sloshing a single drop. "None of this will do any good, Sensei. You're in the blast zone. You will die. The supplies will vaporize. None of this will help anybody."

But not everything in Nagasaki vaporized. I remembered the photos I saw at the library. Some buildings, statues, and other things survived, sometimes even fragile things. Stuff that had cover.

Sensei said, "But I will fail if I think myself more important than the people working outside right now. Those who risked and suffered at my suggestion."

"But you will die!" Alex shouted.

"I may die," Sensei responded. Though his voice was calm and even, if carried no less weight than Alex.

"You will!"

"I may," Sensei said again. He was right. The future wasn't set, no matter how much it might seem that way. This whole mess was happening because things could be changed. I couldn't stop the bomb, but a whisper of an idea was inside of me, trying to figure out how to become a shout.

"You will. The space here is bare, scorched earth before lunch tomorrow. Nothing here will survive."

"Wait," I said.

"Even if that is so, your continued existence shows why that matters less than many other things," Sensei said.

It came to me then, in a flash of realization. I almost shouted, "there's a ridgeline."

"What?" Alex said.

"*Nani*?" Sensei said.

"There's a ridgeline. At the edge of the city. History says the bomb misses its target and falls...will fall... on the other side. It makes a shadow of safety, and the cave we found is on this side of the shadow. What if we moved everything, and everybody we could, into that cave?"

They both stared at me. First, it was the way Fiel and Galhardo did when I tried to make a pun, but then Sensei smiled. And then Alex-Sensei smiled. They looked at each other, and nodded in unison.

Alex said, "Okay. Yes. That would work." She drained her cup, set it down, and looked to Sensei. "Do this, Sensei. Please."

Sensei sat back down. His cup was already empty, but he turned it upside down and set it on the table next to Alex's.

"Yes," he said. "That is good."

CHAPTER 39

Sensei stood back up. With a nod to me and a slight bow to Alex, he stepped outside. Alex made an after you motion and I went next, feeling the reassuring presence of my friend behind me. I stumbled forward on wobbling, exhausted legs.

People outside were standing in the street, milling around and waiting for...well, for something. They still held bundles of clothing, bags of food, and boxes with supplies of all kinds. When we came out, they all stopped talking and looked up at the three of us.

Sensei spoke in Japanese, *"Watashitachi wa minna imasugu ugokanakereba narimasen."*

In my ear, Alex translated, "We must all act quickly."

"Kōgeki ga arimasu. Hiroshima no yōna."

"There will be an attack. Like the one in Hiroshima."

The crowd shook as one, like a single, huge, and frightened being. They murmured to one another with sounds I couldn't understand but that still carried a dread I had known for most of my life. I'd felt that dread every time Mom gave me bad news about moving, or about my dad going to jail again, or about him getting out of jail just as things had started to go right. Tears welled in my eyes, and I just let them flow.

"Onegai, yujin."

"Please, friends," Alex whispered to me.

Gasps sounded, and shouts of fear. I could tell I wasn't the only person crying. A current of real panic rolled through the crowd, so strong I could feel it even without my powers.

"Onegai, yujin."

At the edges of the crowd, people started moving. Those closed to us surged forward, while at the other edges some ran into the night. Sensei raised his hands, palms out, pleading for calm with his words, his face, his body. The crowd ignored him. In their terror, it was like they couldn't even see he was there.

Sensei nodded to himself, then stood straight and breathed deeply. He clapped his hands and rubbed them together in a motion like he had during the earlier battle, only it was gentle and carried a lightness with it. When his power blew past me, it was like smelling a baby, or feeling a soap bubble pop on my cheek. I smiled at the warmth it sent through me, and thought of my mother's smile.

The first time I had felt Sensei do this, it was thunder. This time it was a light, cool rain at the end of a hot afternoon. I saw it work through the crowd. Children quieted. Mothers dried their eyes. Fathers stood straighter under their burdens. Everybody looked up at Sensei, quiet, anticipating, and for the moment unafraid.

They didn't know what they were ready for, but they were ready. Sensei had been right earlier. A warrior isn't just a fighter. A warrior is a leader who people look to when they're certain how to...well, um...when they're not certain.

Sensei rattled out instructions to the crowd, so quickly Alex just shrugged and pointed at what happened next. Three men, older than Alex but younger than Sensei, climbed the stairs. They joined the children's bucket brigade, loading out supplies to men and women at the base of the steps. A seemingly endless throng of hands and arms took the loads and distributed them. Sensei led Alex and I past the line and back into the dojo.

Inside, Sensei selected a small cardboard suitcase. He grabbed a scroll, a tattered book, and a sheaf of letters and photos. He placed them gently inside, nodded to himself, then closed and latched the suitcase. He turned to leave, taking a wooden walking stick with him as he stepped down the stairs and moved toward the other side of the crowd.

I followed him. As we passed the stairs, I said, "What about *Ah* and *Um*?"

"They are...durable," Sensei said. "Do not worry about them." He said something in Japanese to Alex, which she didn't translate for me. They both laughed.

When we reached the back of the crowd, Sensei kept walking. Behind us, people with loaded arms followed us through the park, up the lane, and toward the trail that would lead us all to safety.

CHAPTER 40

When we reached the edge of the jungle, Sensei turned to me. "Move back through the line, please, *Chuugi*. Help whoever needs your help."

"How should I help them?" I asked.

"You will know."

"How will I know?"

He shrugged, and gestured toward the line. It was long, with more than a hundred men, women, and children visible before it snaked around a corner and out of sight. I shrugged, too, and jogged back the way we had come despite the wobble of fatigue I'd felt for so long I considered it a friend.

I saw a mother with three small children, and took her sack of turnips to empty her hands.

I saw two children younger than seven struggling with a box of bandages, and I set it to balance on my head.

I found a family struggling with tins of water, an elderly woman with a backpack bigger than she was, and a child by himself, dragging a sack of rice behind him.

I couldn't help as many people as I wanted to, and I couldn't help those people as much as I wished, but I was big, and strong, and well-fed. When I got back to the front of the line, Alex and Sensei laughed out loud. I must have looked like…well, uh…like somebody carrying thirty or forty boxes and bags of supplies, stumbling up a jungle trail in the middle of the night.

"What are you doing, *Chuugi*?" Alex said. She punched me on the shoulder, and I almost fell under my carefully balanced load.

"I'm helping," I grunted. "Sensei said to help."

"Come on, buddy. That's not helping. That's showing off."

"But they're all so small, and so hungry. And I'm not."

Alex raised her eyebrows in the way she does when I surprise her by saying something smarter than she expects of me. Sensei grunted and said, "Warriors often get the best in times of war."

"We pay the price, though," Alex responded. Her face looked old. Even older than it already was.

"Yes," said Sensei. "Yes we do."

Shouting came from down the line, and a child's scream. I dropped my parcels as carefully as I could and ran to join Sensei and Alex, who were already steps ahead of me.

I hadn't realized how much the parcels weighed until I set them on the ground. Somehow, that realization made me even more tired, despite having unloaded my burdens. But I had somewhere to go when this was over, somewhere that wouldn't be on fire and filled with death and pain. Arms aching and lead in my legs, I turned and ran toward the screaming.

Around the first bend of the trail, three soldiers stood in the way of a family in line. They weren't One-Arm and his group, but were just as thin and their uniforms just as threadbare. They didn't look like monsters, or bad guys. They looked hungry, and afraid. Sensei and Alex stood nearby, with all three barrels pointed at them. I slipped into position just behind the largest of the soldiers, one with rank markings on his shoulder.

The leader shouted, "*Sokode tomare!*" and jabbed toward Sensei with his bayonet. He was still out of reach, but only just barely.

"*Tomodachi, kiite,*" Sensei said. His voice was as strong and calm as always. He smiled gently, looking like a harmless old man.

The Sergeant held his rifle steady, the bayonet pointing directly at Sensei's heart. His soldiers raised their rifles.

None of them had seen me yet. I slipped toward the shadows next to the trail, crouching into a wrestling stance. If things went bad, I could tackle two guards and knock all three of us into another one. That would take enough guns out of the situation for Alex and Sensei to handle the rest.

I hoped.

While the soldiers postured and Sensei spoke in a quiet, even voice, Alex caught my eye. She shook her head slightly, just once. I relaxed, but not so much that I couldn't unrelax if things went the wrong way.

Sensei's voice was still soft, calm, and friendly. "*O tomodachi watashi no tomodachi, kiite.*" He spoke softly and quickly then, and as he spoke something changed in all of the soldiers.

All at once, they dropped their weapons and ran toward the front of the line. By the time I got back up there, they were leading the way, loaded up with all the packages I had been carrying.

I had to laugh. When Alex caught up with me, I asked her, "What did Sensei tell them?"

"The truth."

I gave her side-eye until she relented. "He said we were friends, and they should listen to that friendship."

We reached the cave not long after that. My battle with the other *Chuugi* earlier had toppled all the stone piles. The floor was now a mostly smooth surface, like the bottom of a fast-flowing stream.

A woman arrived, walking beside Alex. She looked older than Mrs. D, and couldn't have weighed more than 70 pounds, but she was lugging a sack the size of a large child. I took it from her, and put it in the pile growing at the center of the cave.

As soon as I set it down, I ran back along the line and loaded myself with more bundles. I gathered thirty before I ran out of things to hold them with or hang them on. Legs and arms aching, I ran them up to the cave, let the people already there take them off of me, then reversed my direction and ran back down the line.

I found a family carrying a chest that probably weighed more than all of them combined. With their help, I hoisted it onto my back and ran it to the cave.

The next time, I gathered sacks from twenty-two children before I lost count. I ran them back to the cave, then turned around again.

My legs burned. My joints creaked under the loads. My breath came in a weird rhythm I'd never heard before. I kept moving. Not everybody in the line would make it to shelter before the bomb came, but somewhere down that line was a person who could move quickly enough to be saved if only they weren't carrying extra weight. The more people I took parcels from, the more likely I was to reach that person.

I took a stack of boxes from an old man with a bent back, and he picked up his grandchild instead. The old wood dug painfully into my arms and left splinters in my hands, but I trudged up the hill with them as fast as my legs would pump.

One man was carrying a dirty blanket, and I had three families pile everything in their arms on it. Then I dragged it behind me like a sled. It was so heavy I felt like it was fighting me the whole time, but I got it to the cave. Dozens of hands helped to unload it before I turned around again.

I was so tired. Every part of me hurt, but I focused on the job in front of me. Nothing existed anymore but the road, and the bundles, and the faces of people I hoped I was helping. I don't always know what to do. Heck, I usually don't know. But I was in 1945, fighting a war against demons older than time, and the faster I moved, the more I carried, the more people would survive this particular battle. It was a simple job, and one I was made to do. So I would keep doing it until Sensei, or Alex, or my own body made me stop.

The line was long, filled with people following the lead of others who had followed Sensei. It still stretched all the way back into town even as I heard morning birds begin to cheep.

I don't know how many loads I had taken before the soldiers came to meet me. It took most of them to lift what I was carrying alone, but by then I was glad for the help.

They took a basket full of blankets from me, and my shoulders almost cried from the relief.

They took a family's suitcases and sacks out of my hands, and I rejoiced in the temporary reprieve.

They took load after load from me, and each time the pain and exhaustion eased just enough for me to turn back and find another load to take on. Finally, as five of them took a steamer trunk from where it balanced on my head, Alex put a hand on my shoulder. She held on even as I turned to run back down the line.

"Time to go, *Chuugi*," she said.

"Just one more," I said. I tried to turn and go further, but my legs gave out from under me. Alex slipped my arm around her shoulders, holding me upright until I could steady my shaking legs.

"No," she said. "It's time to go."

I nodded, wanting to cry. What if I had missed somebody? What if it was one of the children just around the bend? Would it be my fault they died, just so I could save my own life?

We walked to Sensei together, and he understood without words. He hugged us both, one with each arm, and whispered, "If I had listened earlier, we could have saved so many more. Their deaths will ride my spirit. Remember this, *Chuugi*. Remember this, Alex-Sensei. Senseis make mistakes, too."

I closed my eyes and felt the warmth of his presence, his strong arms around us both. Even in such dire moments, his confidence and kindness filled me with warmth and renewed my energy.

"Now," Sensei said as he released us, "go."

"Sensei..." I began, but he cut me off.

"Go!"

In the background, over the noise of the crowd, the birds, and the jungle, I imagined I could hear the drone of an airplane. That couldn't really be possible, but I still felt like I heard it. I looked over to Alex. She was fiddling with the sonic screwdriver. She glanced at me, nodded once, and jogged back down the path.

CHAPTER 41

I don't know how it was possible, but somehow my ruined legs carried me faster down the path than they had before. It was like they'd forgotten how to get tired, or just stopped communicating their exhaustion to me after being ignored for so long.

Can legs give you the silent treatment? Either way, they carried me steady and swiftly down the line of people. Despite my help, hundreds shuffled under their burdens in a line that stretched all the way back to the city. Here in the shadow of the ridge line, many wouldn't have to be in the actual cave to receive some shelter, some protection.

But somewhere on our run, Alex and I would pass the last person to reach a safe distance. Every single man, woman, and child after that person would die in nuclear fire. And if we didn't get to the last gate in time, we would die with them.

I stumbled at the thought, nearly taking a header and tumbling down the mountainside. When I shifted my weight to catch myself, my right knee buckled from the load. Three wobbling steps kept me upright, but only barely. I would have to put those thoughts away, and think about them later. If I let them get to me now, I would become one of the dead.

I had done what I could in the time I had. The bomb was coming. Some people would be alive tomorrow who would not have been had I not carried their things. That would have to be enough.

Over the beat of my heart, which I could see in my eyes and feel in my fingers, a sound arose from the predawn sky: the steady drone of an airplane engine. This time, I knew it was real.

Alex was right in front of me, and I shouted to her through my raw throat. "Do you hear that?"

"Those are the escort fighters. The Enola Gay is right behind them."

"How long do we have?"

"Five minutes."

As we raced through the cold morning city, I realized something had changed. I didn't know how many turns back. Somewhere in the haze of it all, we had reached and passed the end of the line of people following Sensei to safety. I couldn't help them now.I could only hope that some of them, even just one, would live through the next hour because I had helped.

Sometimes all you can do has to be enough. I hoped I could keep believing that if we made it through the gate in time. I called to Alex, "How soon to the gate?"

"Three minutes."

"Good," I panted. I urged more speed out of my legs. Though I couldn't actually feel if they were moving faster, the buildings on either side of me seemed to slip by more quickly. "I eat pressure for breakfast. I eat it for lunch. I order big buckets of it at the movie theater instead of popcorn." Then I realized something else. "Alex!"

"Yeah?" my friend shouted without turning her head.

I panted, "There...aren't...any...*oni*...anywhere."

"They know what's coming," Alex's voice came smoothly. She'd always been the better runner. "They're hiding."

Two corners later, we came on something just as bad as a street full of demons. One-Arm and three other soldiers stood in the street, surrounding a family with two small children. Ears and Pimples searched through a sack, pulling out food and throwing it into a pile at the father's feet.

Alex growled, "Of course, not all devils are smart enough to come in when the light is on its way."

Ears threw an empty jar to shatter at the older child's feet. She leapt, and started to cry. Even in the dim morning light, I could see the soldier smile like...well, like a person who likes to hurt people. Like my dad sometimes did when he was drunk and sad, and would say things to make Mom sad, too.

There was no shelter to be had here. Every single one of them, soldiers and family alike, would be dead in less than four minutes. They would all be dead. I couldn't save the little girl, or her baby brother. But I could let them spend their last minutes on earth hugging their family. They wouldn't have to die in fear, harassed by bullies who would turn into cinders at the same time they did.

That didn't mean everything, and maybe it didn't really mean anything. But it was important to me in that moment. I knew that if a time ever came where I couldn't save Mom, I would want her to spend the last seconds of that time hugging me.

I sped up to come beside Alex and catch her eye. She understood without my saying a word.

"High card special?"

"What's a high card special?"

She sighed. "I hit the leader in the legs and you jump-kick his face."

"Oh," I smiled at the thought of it. "Okay."

All four soldiers were distracted tormenting the family, so they didn't hear us until it was way too late. Alex did a rolling sweep to One-Arm's legs. While he was falling, I jump-kicked him in the neck. He went down like he had an off button.

The other soldiers froze, stunned, staring at the unmoving form of their boss. Alex dropped two of them with almost invisibly fast kicks to the head while I threw the last through the wall of a crumbling building nearby. I pointed at the family, all four of them staring wide-eyed at Alex and me. We must have looked like demons to them with our size, and Alex's pale skin. Then I pointed to the thickest, strongest-looking building I could see. Maybe it would be enough.

"Two minutes, buddy," Alex said. "Time to go." She translated my pantomimed instructions to the family while I reached down to pick up one of the rifles the soldiers had dropped.

"Leave it," Alex said.

"Why?"

"How good of a shot are you?"

I dropped the gun. As I straightened up, a hot, dry wind washed over us. It pulled at our clothes, and the banners hanging from the few intact eaves nearby.

A single sheet of paper flew by me on the breeze. On it was a photo of a young girl tying a headband over her forehead. She wore a look of fierce pride in her eyes and gripped a wooden spear in both hands.

I thought for a second that we were too late, and the wind was the lead of the blast wave. But no, I could still hear the bomber. It was coming closer, not moving away.

Then I saw where the wind was coming from. Up the road behind us, the other *Chuugi* was running at us so fast he was pushing the air in front of him. His swords gleamed in each hand, ready to cut us both in half.

CHAPTER 42

We turned and ran, gaining distance slightly despite how my legs kept threatening to turn to jelly with every step. At this point, they were somehow completely numb but also on fire with pain. That didn't seem fair, but I only had to use them for another ninety seconds. After that, it would be over.

One way or the other.

A *tanuki* jumped down from a roof, landing on my head. I threw myself into a shoulder roll and peeled it off of me onto the street where Alex stomped its head. The move was quick, but cost us some distance. An upward glance told me more were in the shadows.

"I thought," I gasped, "You said they were taking cover?"

Alex swatted a diving demon out of our way. The sound of the bomber was a constant buzz echoing through the city. "Well, maybe these ones aren't need to know?"

More *tanuki* rained down on us from above. None of them got a lasting hold on us, but every single one broke our stride. I could feel *Chuugi* getting closer with each shadow creature he sacrificed to us. There was a lesson there, how Sensei refused to leave the city to save himself while my evil twin sent dozens of his minions to their deaths just for a chance to kill me and Alex. But whatever lesson that was would have to wait. The sound of the bomber filled the air.

Beneath its buzz, pounding footsteps in close pursuit thundered toward us. He was gaining, but we didn't have time for another stand-up battle. We had to beat him to the gate if we wanted to avoid the apocalypse that was going to fall from the heavens in just minutes. Alex spun on her heel and reversed direction, running as fast as she could toward the giant warrior. I tried to spin as well, but my leg gave out and I fell onto my bottom, skidding along the cobblestones. By the time I was up, she was inches from a collision with the gigantic warrior.

Chuugi was by far more powerful, bigger than me and much stronger, but Alex wasn't picking a head-on fight. She directed her attack to catch him in one hip, spinning him around with his own inertia and power. The warrior fell on his face and skidded like a derailed train into a house with most of its roof still intact. The tiles fell, along with the rest of the house, completely burying him.

Even as I turned to face the charging lesser demons, I was sure I'd seen the rubble move. He probably couldn't dig himself out from under the rubble before we were gone, but I wasn't going to stick around to find out.

Alex tried to stand, but collapsed onto her face. Whatever force she'd put into *Chuugi* to make him fall had hit her just as hard. I sprinted up and slung her over my shoulders.

"How long do we have?"

"Fifty seconds."

"How far now?"

She moved, taking out her sonic screwdriver and checking. "Forty-five seconds."

I dug deep, running hard through the rubble-strewn streets. Nobody was out, the entire city silent like it was holding its breath in anticipation of what would come next.

I crested a small rise to see the gate already fully formed, its center open wide to show the cool, well-lit locker room on the other side. Hundreds of *oni* crouched on the benches and lockers, waiting for us. But they were a problem for later. Between it and us were at least twenty soldiers, with more than twice that many *oni* dancing on their shoulders, riding their backs, and squirming around their legs.

I didn't even slow down. Couldn't slow down even if I wanted to. With Alex feeling like she was my size on my shoulders, I narrowed my focus on the gate until it was the only thing I could see. Nothing could distract me if we were going to make it in time. I gripped my friend tight to me and ran at the smallest soldier in the line with everything I had left in me. Somewhere overhead I heard the droning buzz of the bomber, so loud now it felt like it had to be over the city.

I imagined I heard the whistling noise falling bombs make in cartoons, but that couldn't be possible. Bombs didn't actually make that sound when they fell, and it would be too far away for me to hear if I did. What I absolutely could hear was a crash of timber and a roar of fury a few hundred feet behind me. *Chuugi* was getting up, despite the weight of a house on top of him.

The bomber's drone changed its pitch from high to low the same way a police siren will when the car passes you. I remembered from science class that was called the Doppler effect, and realized it meant the bomber had passed directly overhead. It was leaving the city, meaning they had dropped the bomb.

I hadn't thought I had anything more left in my tank in that moment, but that sound and what it meant proved me wrong. I did have a little extra, and I put every bit of it on the line.

Bone and muscle crunched as I slammed through a guard with all the combined weight of me and Alex. He went down like I'd hit him with a car. Gunfire sounded two steps later, followed by a heavy impact against my back. I thought I'd been shot, but the pain didn't come. Instead I felt a wet warmth soaking into the back of my shirt.

Alex-Sensei.

Ahead of me glowed brightly purple in the morning sun.

Blinding white light flashed behind us, bringing with it a terrible heat. I half-leapt, half-rode the wave into and through the gate, so hurting and tired and terrified that traveling through time felt like merciful relief.

CHAPTER 43

We landed in the locker room floor, Alex screaming on top of me and a light I didn't dare look at shining behind us. I rolled up, leaving my wounded friend safe on the ground, to face the horde of oni waiting for us. They had seemed smaller, and less numerous, viewed through the center of the gate.

The blast wave had knocked back or taken out some of the demons, so I had enough space to stand up before they piled onto me. I kicked and tore at them, but there were too many. I fell to my knees under their weight.

"Alex!" I shouted, but she wasn't moving. I rolled to cover her body with mine as more demons surrounded us. Their claws tore at me and their evil, chittering voices filled my brain with thoughts so dark and cold they made me wish I had burned in the blast 80 years before.

I roared my way to my feet, throwing *oni* off of myself in a spray of shadowy forms. I grabbed one in each hand and used them to bludgeon the others away until both popped into nothingness under the blows. Others flew into me from all sides, sending me stumbling. I slammed into a toilet stall, through the swinging metal door. My hands flew to the sides, catching me before I could fall and slam my head on something cold, hard, and unforgiving.

Everything hurt, everywhere. I couldn't even tell which pain came from all I had done to my body already, and which came from new attacks. Something dark and heavy, with feathery skin, landed on my head and wrenched me down to my knees. I was so tired. Too tired to fight them even if I wasn't already wounded.

I leaned for support against the stall wall as even more of them piled into the tight space. Something heavy hit me in my gut and I fell to one knee. The demons cackled in glee as they felt my weakness grow. It echoed in my ears and scratched at my mind and spirit. I screamed defiance, but my voice shook.

Out the door of the stall, Alex lay motionless on the floor. None of the *oni* were on her, instead focused on defeating me. At least that was something. The relief I felt only sucked more energy out of me. There were so many of them, and they were so heavy. Another pair of paws landed on my shoulders and dug in with short, sharp talons. A slimy, scaly tail wrapped around my neck.

The choke rallied me for just a second. Waves of panic brought the adrenaline, and I rolled left and right to shake the monsters off of me like a bear fighting dogs. I fought dirty then, gouging flesh off of them with my own fingers like claws. I bit and elbowed. I thumbed out eyes when I could find them, and flesh off faces when I couldn't.

My dad used to say, "If it's worth fighting, it's worth fighting dirty." I didn't often get a chance to use my dad's advice, and when I did it was almost never a good idea. Dirty fighting, Dirty language. Dirty living. That's a part of him I don't want to be a part of me. But in those few seconds when I thought I was going to survive, I took his advice to heart and tore into the *oni* with every dirty trick I had. And for those few seconds, I thought it would be enough.

But it wasn't. Something dug its claws into the back of my knee and I went down hard. When it released me, there was more weight on my head than I could handle. I was on the floor, my face flat against the tile, pressed down so hard I couldn't breathe.

I put my palms flat on the ground. One pushup. One single pushup and I could breathe again. I didn't have it in me, but this wasn't the first time I'd managed a pushup when my tank was empty. If I could make it happen, it wouldn't be the last.

My arms shook and trembled, my muscles shuddered, my legs screamed, but I raised myself up. The *oni* pulled and scratched my arms, driving me back down. My nose stung as it hit the ground with a crack, and the dozens of demons on my head pressed my face into the tile.

Just one more pushup. I almost made it all the way up before they pulled my arms out again. Their weight pressed my face into the tile and closed off my mouth and nose. Stars danced in my vision and the edges of my world went black.

Just one pushup. I got just enough distance to take in a raw, gasping breath.

Just one.

It was no good. I had nothing left.

Another monster jumped onto my head, pressing my face into the hard tile until my mouth and nose were sealed. I tried to rise, tried even to roll, but I had nothing. There was nothing left. No more.

No more pushups.

No more fight.

No more Mom, or Bushido Warriors, or scholarships.

No more.

CHAPTER 44

I heard a faint thump, and a slightly less faint squeal of pain. Then nothing was on my head. I lifted my face and sucked in air. The world got less distant, and I could hear louder and louder sounds of mayhem as the rest of the weight came off my body.

I pushed myself to my knees, using the stall walls for support, forcing my vision to unblur so I could find Alex. I hoped trying to kill me had kept all the *oni* occupied enough that she would still be all right. I found her, still facedown on the floor near some benches, with the other Alex standing with one foot on either side of her.

Alex, my Alex, not a sensei yet but a teenager like me, stood like some primal goddess of wrath and love, visiting violence upon our enemies. As I struggled to my feet, she swept low with one leg to send a half-dozen demons spinning like black, evil tops. When they struck walls or lockers, they exploded into nothingness.

I tried to take a step forward, but my legs weren't up to it yet. I gripped the stall walls and watched while Alex danced in a small circle, keeping her older self out of reach from the demons she was annihilating.

A wave of demons came at her from all sides, colliding on her position like a swirling tide but somehow just missing her with every swipe and bite. With light touches, she directed their flying bodies, sending them crashing into the hardest edges of the locker room. A spider with bat wings exploded against the corner of a sink. A fat rabbit with giant fangs slammed into a concrete wall. A deep black butterfly splattered against the tusks of a tiny rhinoceros with eleven eyes.

I tried another step, and my legs held that time. I moved forward to join the fight, to help my friend despite my exhaustion. Without breaking stride, Alex skipped across the floor and kicked me gently in the chest. I backpedaled from the push until my knees hit the toilet and I fell onto my butt, watching through the open doorway.

My friend had cut down the demons' numbers, but still they came in. She stood without flinching, her whole body daring the next to take another step forward, a fierce and knowing courage flashing in her eyes. She shifted an inch to avoid raking claws, then spun to slam and turn their wielder into a memory with a vicious elbow strike. Alex faced them all, unafraid and eerie in her power.

One brave or stupid *oni*, a fat blob with a face like a minotaur, charged at Alex. She punted it like a football for a perfect goal through the stall door and into my hands. I turned, shoved it into the toilet, and closed the lid over its squeals. I sat back down and flushed until I heard it pop out of existence.

When I looked back up, the oni were gone. Alex stood alone, breathing deeply and looking beautiful and strong, the way Mom looks in my mind no matter how hard life has tried to make her look weak or ugly. She scanned the room once more, drew her hands together so one palm wrapped around her closed fist, and bowed, once, to...I didn't know. Maybe to herself? Maybe to the people who had taught her? Then she raised her head and gave me the same smile she wore when we all played *Cards Against Humanity* at Sage's house.

I struggled out toward Alex. We high-fived, then knelt by Alex-Sensei's side. Well, Alex knelt. I mostly flopped to a kneeling position.

"Alex-Sensei?" I said. Alex looked to me, then to our friend.

Her eyes opened, though she was bleeding and her breath seemed weak. I shifted so she could lay her head in my lap. Her eyes widened as she saw who I was with, and she gave a gasp that turned into wracking coughs.

When she had settled enough to speak, she whispered, "I have to think that's not good."

"Hi, Alex," my Alex said.

"Hi, Alex," Alex-Sensei said, then to me, "She knows?"

"She helped me figure out how to use the sonic screwdriver."

Alex said, "He has no idea why you call it that, does he?"

Alex-Sensei just laughed, chuckling harder and harder. The other Alex joined her.

As they calmed down, Alex-Sensei said to my Alex, "I never realized how beautifully we fought."

Alex blushed. I scanned the room for more demons, but we were alone. She had destroyed or driven off every one of the monsters that had almost killed me. She really was the best fighter of us all, despite being half my size.

Alex dropped to her knees beside her counterpart, her fingers moving lightly over her body, probing for injuries and signs of damage. She whispered to herself, "That's not good. Need to stop the bleeding. Is that a bullet wound? You realize this is our body?"

She had me set Alex-Sensei's head on the ground and scoot out of the way. As she slid to kneel at her head, she stared past her and her eyes widened.

"Holy shit. Is that what I think it is?"

I followed her gaze to the wall of the locker room. In a perfect circle, the paint had been burned off down to the concrete, leaving the cinder blocks exposed and bleached nearly white. At the circle's center was the shadow of a large figure carrying a small one over its shoulders, the two of them leaping toward something the image didn't show.

"Woah," Alex-Sensei said.

"Yeah," said Today Alex. "Woah."

We sat together and regarded what was there. I had no words for what it meant, or what it did to me to see it. Apparently, neither did either Alex. The PA system was the next thing to make a noise in that room.

"Connor Morgan to Mat 7. Last call for Connor Morgan to Mat 7." My stomach clenched and my legs cramped in anticipation of further exhaustion.

"What time is it?' I said, my breath already coming short.

Alex-Sensei glanced at the sonic screwdriver, "A little after ten in the morning."

"What day is it?"

Present Alex said, "Friday."

"That's my death match," I said.

"Your what now?" my Alex asked. Her voice was somewhere between amused and exasperated, which was about normal for her when dealing with me.

"Never mind," I answered. "I mean to change it."

CHAPTER 45

I tried to stand, and had to try twice more before my legs would hold my weight. Alex grabbed my arm and pulled me to sit on a bench.

"You can't wrestle, *Chuugi*. You can hardly stand."

"But I have to," I said. "Don't I, Alex-sensei?" I almost just said Alex, but caught myself just in time. These things weren't getting less weird, but I was getting a little better at dealing with it.

"I don't know," said Today-Alex anyway.

"No," Alex-Sensei said from her place on the floor. She was still lying down, blood staining her clothes where the bullet had grazed her, and all across her arms and right leg. While I'd been feeling sorry for myself about being so tired, Alex-Sensei had suffered serious wounds without a single sound of complaint.

"Wait, what?" Today-Alex and I said together.

"There are three of you in this here-now," Alex croaked. Her eyelids flitted shut, but her voice stayed strong. "One of the other versions of you will do the dying."

"Dothewhatnow?" Alex said, her voice a high-pitched squeak.

"I'll explain," Alex said. "But *Chuugi*, you need to stop it happening."

"How?"

"I don't know, but there is an answer. And it's out there someplace."

I got to my feet on the first try that time, and walked out into the stadium while the Alexes whispered about things that might not be.

Every step was agony and exhaustion. The fluorescent lights in the service hallway didn't just hurt my eyes, they hurt my skin. My legs felt like I was wearing heavy boots of lead.

When I moved through the doors to the colosseum floor, the noise of the crowd hit me like a physical wall. It took me longer than it should have to orient myself and point my aching body in the direction of mat seven.

The crowd was thick, almost too thick to move through as I tried to make my way toward where Coach Russel and Sage were already standing. For a moment, I realized this must be how regular people felt in crowds all the time. As big as I am, I usually just wade through the people and get where I'm headed.

Even though I was still a long way back, I could see mat seven clearly as another version of me stepped onto it across from Angus Brawn, and between us, yet another me arguing with a different Alex-Sensei about whether or not I should watch what came next. Even now, knowing what I knew, I couldn't decide which of us was right.

Everything looked familiar, but I noticed small differences. Angus's uniform had yellow piping that hadn't been there before. The tape wrapping my ankle was blue instead of tan. And Avo, Mrs. D. and Sensei were all there, standing next to Mom as close to the mat as the crowd would allow.

The ref blew the whistle. It echoed strangely in my ears, like a fire alarm in the middle of a fight: its importance was larger than its actual volume. I weaved through the crowd and heard Mom's voice, too. "Make him eat that hand, Connor Morgan!"

The tournament floor was so crowded, I heard the buzzer for the end of the first round by the time I came up behind Avo, Mrs. D., and Sensei. None of them looked confused to see me both behind them and in front of them on the mat. But that made sense. They would remember for the same reasons Alex-Sensei would...and for the same reasons I wouldn't once this was all over. Mom didn't see me standing in the back. She was focused on the me on the mat, looking like she was ready to go out there and put Angus down herself.

As the next round began I watched myself take the down position. I could almost feel the hate and anger radiating off of Angus as he wrapped his arms into position. The buzzer sounded. I rolled and scored my points, the Angus grabbed my face. Coach shouted the ref's name and used the F-word.

It was all happening just as it had before. The little details like Angus's uniform and my elders on the floor didn't matter. I was going to die, and none of what I'd done with Alex was changing that. I'd missed something.

On the mat, Angus rolled us until he was on top. He slammed his foot into the back of my head in a motion that could have looked accidental, but clearly wasn't. The buzzer sounded. Mom stormed out onto the mat with Sage. Angus's coach shouted, "Angus! What the hell are you doing?"

And then I saw it. Off the mat, behind Coach, Sage and Mom, behind Avo, Mrs. D. and Sensei, in a crowd watching the action on mat six, somebody was looking the wrong way.

It's no good to try paying attention to everything at once. The world is too busy and full of things to get anything that way. Instead, Sensei taught us, you have to look for things that stand out. Things that are different from what you expect. In that knot of athletes and coaches watching two kids wrestle on mat six, one of them was looking in the opposite direction. Somebody tall, with buzz-cut black hair and muscles bulging under a UFC t-shirt.

Somebody I'd last seen in Nagasaki, running at us after I'd dropped a house on his head.

It was Mr. Waldron, staring at Angus and muttering words of power under his breath. It was *Chuugi*. The old *Chuugi*. And he was trying to kill me.

CHAPTER 46

My stomach twisted in knots as I glanced between the concentrating warrior and the mat, where the other me was standing up to head back out. I *looked*, seeing what I already knew was there: black tendrils of power writhing between the evil warrior and the athlete, controlling Angus like the strings of a puppet. It had been him all along. *Chuugi* had killed me, and was trying again right now.

The other me walked onto the mat, limping a little but standing tall. The black strings thickened and grew darker. *Chuugi* smiled in a thin line, and a cold I could only feel with my mind frosted out from him.

I sidled out of his field of vision and slipped through the crowd. His concentration was so absolute he didn't see me approaching the knot of people next to Mat Six, as the other me stood to the line. He didn't see me sliding up to him as the whistle blew. He didn't feel me standing just behind him as Angus palm struck my double in the face. The old warrior, the old traitor, was so focused on murdering that me, he didn't sense this me coming within striking distance. Within killing distance. He was mine.

But what could I do about it? I couldn't just kill him, or even attack him. We were surrounded by people, and they would all get involved. The best case would get me disqualified, suspended, maybe put in jail. The worst case would have people see two or even three versions of me before it was all over. I didn't know what that would mean, but no way was that good. And while I stood there thinking of a solution, my murder was coming closer by the instant.

Angus dropped to a knee even as the whistle blew. *Chuugi* smiled wider and the tentacles thickened further. I balled my hands into fists, staring at the vulnerable points at the base of his skull. Just one punch was all it would take.

Angus's coach shouted, "Angus! What the hell are you doing?" Angus pulled me into a fireman's carry. *Chuugi* raised his arms slightly and power pulsed from them toward my opponent, the boy who would soon be my murderer. I stood watching, thinking desperately, with no good options to do or not to do. Everything lead to ruin. Everything led to loss.

Chuugi's arms raised higher and a massive wave of blackness began to build inside him, one I could have felt even without *looking*. I opened my fists and stuck out two fingers of my right hand. Angus lifted me above his head. *Chuugi* radiated hate and triumph.

I tickled him right under his left arm.

The wave of blackness popped like a balloon. *Chuugi* did a whole-body flinch so wild he jostled people to his left and right. Angus sagged like he'd been switched off, and I fell to the mat with a crash that echoed all the way to the ceiling. Heads snapped toward Mat 7 from everywhere, and me — the me on the mat, the me who should be dead — shouted from the pain of landing. He was alive, and I was alive.

Chuugi mastered himself faster than a thought, and whirled to stare at me. Even without his samurai armor, he was huge. He stood a head taller than me, and was as much thicker as I was thicker than Alex. His wide eyes narrowed as he recognized me, and his feet shifted into a ready position. My hand almost moved, almost threw a sharp jab at the huge man's throat. With him facing me, I could claim self-defense. If he fought back, people would see him for who he was. Sensei was just feet away, standing with Alex, and Mr. D., and Avo.

But no. Even as the thought ran through me, *Chuugi* shifted his position a fraction of an inch. The punch would miss, and leave me open. He had felt me just wanting to punch him, and I realized then that he'd had more than half a century to practice and train, while I had only fast-forwarded through those decades.

His face passed from surprise, to rage, to an almost genuine smile. He winked down at me. "Very good, *Chuugi*. You're learning which battles are worth fighting, and which are not."

"So are you," I said. I tried hard to keep my voice steady and confident. "You know you'd lose this one, just like you did in Nagasaki."

He laughed, a mocking sound that didn't match the heat in his eyes or the tightness of his smile. In the background, the PA announced me as the winner of my match. I could hear Mom's and Sage's cheers over the crowd. I had survived and won my match. I smirked at *Chuugi*, and he bowed his head in acknowledgement.

"How do they say it in the movies," he said, "you win this round?" He paused, like he was waiting for me to correct him. When I didn't, he repeated, "You win this round."

"We'll win the next one, too," I told him.

He reached out and grabbed my shoulder, not so tight it hurt but with enough force I would have to work to get loose. "But, *Chuugi*. You won't remember this time. I'll have the advantage of surprise, because I will always, always remember you."

"Won't matter. If you could take us, you would have already. Bring it." I hoped my voice sounded braver than I felt.

Chuugi let go of my shoulder and chucked me under the chin. He seemed to move slowly, but was far too fast for me to stop him. "We'll meet again, kid. Soon. I'm sure you'll figure out which side to be on."

I aimed a rude word in his direction. He laughed and tapped my knee, stomach, and arm so rapidly I hadn't even responded to the first before his hand was in the pocket of his track pants. The pain in each place blossomed, exposing every wound, strain, and sprain I'd gotten in the past days. "That's what your side gets. That pain. Pain is the wages of weakness and indecision. You'll come around in time. I can see it in you."

"Oh yeah?" I tried to come up with something, but was only halfway to even a weak comeback before he turned with a laugh and somehow melted into the crowd. He took just three steps and was gone.

CHAPTER 47

I had to dodge and duck to avoid Fiel, Galhardo, and Susan as they ran through the crowd toward mat seven, probably to congratulate me. It's harder than you think, hiding in a crowd when you're one of the biggest people in the room, but they were focused on the other me.

One of the other mes.

The first thing I saw when I got back to the locker room was my two friends, sitting on a bench together. Today-Alex had bandaged up Alex-Sensei neatly, and was making her drink some kind of mixture from a paper cup. Behind them was the shadow on the wall, a shadow not from light but from time. It was a monument of a kind, to the sacrifices we'd made and to the suffering of all those people I had been too slow to help.

Today-Alex looked up, saw me staring, and followed my gaze to the nuclear shadow. "Yeah," she said. "That was close."

Close for us. I thought about how many people on the other side it was closer, too close, for. History said 80,000 people died that morning. I could only hope Alex and I had made that number a little smaller.

"We're all right?" Alex-Sensei asked.

"I think so," I said. "I'm alive." Every inch of my body hurt that wasn't sotired it couldn't feel anything, but I was all right. "How are you, sister?"

"I think I sprained my pancreas," Alex-Sensei said, but she was smiling. "It's nothing twenty-second century medtech can't fix in a weekend."

"So you're going back?"

"Yes."

Today-Alex said, "What happens now?"

"Sensei survived. So did *Chuugi* here. Things are back to how they are supposed to be."

"You're sure?" I said. "How do we know?"

"I'm not certain how I know," Alex-Sensei admitted. "But I'm certain it's true. It feels right, inside. Like an itch in my soul that doesn't need scratching anymore."

Today-Alex's face was grave. "That's not much."

"True, but it's all we have."

"So you go home," I said, "and then?"

"Well, and remember that I don't know much about this. There should be a time snap."

"A what snap?" I asked. I knew what both of those words meant, but my exhausted mind couldn't make them work together in a way that made sense.

Alex-Sensei looked at me, then spoke to Today-Alex. "I told *Chuugi* earlier how this was all possible because of ripples in the stream of time. We rode the waves those ripples made."

Today-Alex nodded, almost like it made perfect sense.

"You know how if you throw in a big rock, there's a hole in the water?" Alex-Sensei said.

"And then the water crashes into the hole, filling it back in," Today-Alex said. It wasn't a question.

"Yes. Exactly. *Chuugi*, are you getting this?"

I sighed. "As much as I'm likely to, I guess."

"Good," Alex-Sensei said. Today-Alex patted my back gently.

"So, the hole will close, and a lot of things will be as they were before the enemy started messing with time."

"How much of this will we remember?" Today-Alex asked.

"None of it," Alex-Sensei said. As she spoke, the air began to thicken. The hairs on my arms stood on end.

Alex-Sensei noticed it, too. "We have about a minute, I would guess."

I stepped forward, and pulled my friend to her feet. I hugged her tight. She groaned from the pressure on her wounded body, but I didn't let go. Today-Alex wrapped her arms gently around us both.

"This is the last ripple?" I asked.

"Last one, my friend. This will close, and the final temporal tide will wash over you. If I understand things correctly, it will suddenly be a little while ago and everything will be normal."

"And I really won't remember anything?"

"No. You won't. But I will. And Sensei will remember some of it." She looked at us both one more time, and it seemed like she was paler than usual. "Alex, you might have some weird dreams for a while. Then one day, you'll remember it all. You two keep each other safe. It's going to get a lot worse before you meet me."

I squeezed her tighter. This time she didn't groan.

"I wish," she said, "I'd seen Galhardo just one more time."

"You will, sister," I said. "You will. Tell him hi for us. Tell us all hi for us."

Alex squeezed us both hard, then stepped back. She looked like she was trying not to cry. "Goodbye, brother. Goodbye, sister."

The gate appeared again, a tiny point of bright light at the center of its swirling purple disk.

"This may feel...a little weird."

"But will it hurt?" I asked, a smile on my face despite this parting.

"Only a little." She held out her fist for me to bump one last time. When the wave hit us, it didn't hurt at all.

But it did feel a little weird.

CHAPTER 48

I'd made it to Friday.

The Oregon State Wrestling Championships start on Thursday morning. If you lose two matches, you're out. Everybody in it on Friday had a shot at a meal on Saturday night, and a shot at a scholarship. This was good news for me and Mom. The bad news was, I had to wrestle Angus Brawn first thing..

Looking at the giant athlete across the bright red wrestling match, I promised myself I would do better against him than my two-point loss in a dual meet just after Christmas. My friend Sage Kaiser slapped my butt and whispered, "Bring me one of his ears."

I laughed. Behind her, Mom, Mrs. D, Avo, and even Sensei stood in a small knot and cheered. I had no idea how they'd gotten permission to be on the tournament floor, but there they were, smiling. Avo and Mrs. D. were making some kind of chant or cheer in unison, moving their hands like they were dancing. The pattern pulled me into if for a moment, and I stared at it. There was some kind of meaning there, just beyond my ability to see.

"No," Sage said, pulling my attention back to the match.. "I'm serious. You come off that mat and he has both of his ears, I'm stealing your lunch money." She slapped my butt again. The referee called me forward, and I walked out to meet Angus. He shook my hand and the ref blew the whistle.

I faked high and dove low for a clean double-leg takedown. Angus hit the ground with a loud crunch and a satisfying grunt. The ref raised two fingers to call my score. I smiled as the scorekeeper put my points up on the board. I couldn't quite keep Angus on his back long enough to score near-fall points, but I kept the pressure on and he stayed flat on his belly. He might have been tough, but he wasn't going anywhere.

Things were looking good. Who knew what the future had in store?

The End

ABOUT THE AUTHOR

Jason Brick began his lifelong martial arts habit with wrestling in 7th grade. The discipline he learned there is why he has what it takes to write for a living today. When not writing or training, he cooks and spoils his family. He lives in Oregon.